SHELTER

SHELTER

Benette Whitmore

WALKER & COMPANY
NEW YORK

First published in the United States of America in 2006 by
Walker Publishing Company, Inc.
Distributed to the trade by Holtzbrinck Publishers

For information about permission to reproduce selections from
this book, write to Permissions, Walker & Company,
104 Fifth Avenue, New York, New York 10011

Library of Congress Cataloging-in-Publication Data
Whitmore, Benette.
Shelter / Benette Whitmore.
p. cm.
Summary: When sixteen-year-old Skyler's teacher tells her to make a video diary the
summer her mother builds a bomb shelter in the backyard, Sky chronicles her twin
brother's increasing drug use, her strained relationship with her best friend when a boy
enters the picture, and her mother's bad choice of a new boyfriend.
ISBN-10: 0-8027-8884-X · ISBN-13: 978-0-8027-8884-9
[1. Fallout shelters—Fiction. 2. Twins—Fiction. 3. Brothers and sisters—Fiction.
4. Drug abuse—Fiction. 5. Single-parent families—Fiction. 6. Video recordings—
Fiction. 7. Diaries—Fiction.] I. Title.
PZ7.W5985Sh 2006   [Fic]—dc22   2006001972

Book design by Nicole Gastonguay

Visit Walker & Company's Web site at www.walkeryoungreaders.com

Printed in the United States of America.

2 4 6 8 10 9 7 5 3 1

All papers used by Walker & Company are natural, recyclable products
made from wood grown in well-managed forests. The manufacturing processes
conform to the environmental regulations of the country of origin.

FOR KALLIE & MAXXANN

WITH THANKS TO
Emily Easton (The Queen of Wands)
for your patience & clarity

Patrick Lawler (The Magician)
for your friendship & guidance

Tom McGrath (The Knight of Cups)
for your love & inspiration, always

Scene 1

It's where I lost my virginity and also my mind.

In that order.

But then I got it back again.

My mind, that is.

Driving by the house, no one would have believed it. Just a three-bedroom raised ranch: a perfect specimen of the all-American dream.

923 Hyde Road.

"Your place has character," our mailman, Conrad, said more than twice.

Grass mowed weekly in a diagonal format, per my mother's

instructions. Hedges trimmed semimonthly. Clapboards painted ice cap blue. A blacktop driveway sealed yearly, orange warning ties dangling from a string.

It didn't exist when we bought the house, way before I was even born.

Mom made the announcement at a family meeting, which besides her included the sum total of my brother Will and me.

MOM: I've hired some contractors, to do a special project. It's a little more involved than the deck was.

WILL: Mom, can you speed this up? The guys are waiting.

Will was as jumpy as the paint mixer at Home Depot.

MOM: It's a room underground. I figure we need it, just in case.

ME: In case of what?

MOM: In case of never mind. I really don't think we'll ever need it, we probably won't even use it, but it'll make us feel good. Just knowing it's there.

WILL: If we don't need it, if we won't use it, then why don't we get something else, like a boat or a Ski-doo or a new car?

Will and I traded smiles. A silent high five.

MOM: I've already signed the papers. They're starting work tomorrow night.

ME: Tomorrow night? As in, when it's dark?

MOM: Well, yes, we've decided it's best for them to work at night. We certainly don't want to alarm the neighbors, Skyler.

I scanned my family and took a mental snapshot, searched for images I needed to depict the Baxter family backstory.

How do I explain my mother? For one thing, she hides her valuables in a fake head of lettuce in the refrigerator crisper. She ordered it off the Home Shopping Network. "What robber would ever suspect a leafy vegetable?" she said, glowing like the refrigerator light. Well, any unemployed robber who's home watching the Home Shopping Network, for one, I thought. But I just stared at her instead. Maybe if I looked long enough, that fuzzy picture I had of her would somehow come into focus.

Then there was Will Jr., my sorta big brother. Only by six minutes, though. He took his sorry time getting himself out, so he almost didn't have a little sister. But Mom says I kicked him out just in time.

"The doctor said sixty more seconds and I don't know what," my mother told me.

Thanks for sharing *that* cheerful thought, Mom.

Benette Whitmore

I know most brothers and sisters don't get along, Sometimes twins can't stand each other, but Will and me, we've always had this connection. After all, we were hanging out together for almost nine months with no place to go.

What's the alternative?

I taught Will how to talk, so says my mother. She said I was his interpreter; only I could understand his babbles. And that stands true today.

As in, Will still needs some serious explaining. Some explaining that too often exceeds my own scope of understanding. Not that I don't try to take a stab at it when it comes to helping him out, which often includes protecting him at all costs from the appropriate authority figure at hand. The appropriate authority figure who is mainly Mom.

Lucky for Will she is way too nice and cool, the kind of mother every teenager wishes they had. And also lucky for Will she is her happiest when she's living in the Land of Denial.

Not so lucky for me. Me, who is too young to be the parent, especially the parent of my own twin brother.

Especially when my own twin brother is Will.

Will could write a memoir featuring all of his indiscretions that led to Trouble with a capital *T.* Now you may wonder, why make trouble when you don't need to? Good question, if you ask me. Keep things on the down low, that's always been my personal philosophy. But on the flip-flop of that logical perspective is Will, which leads to his lengthy rap sheet that includes but is not limited to

1. Sneaking out his bedroom window to be front and center at each and every miscellaneous keg party taking place within the Red Creek County limits. (Caught.)
2. Hiding a bottle of hard stuff in his locker at school. (Caught.)
3. Growing a pot garden under the bleachers adjacent to the high school athletic field. (Caught.)

Anybody notice a pattern here?

I spend way too much of my so-called carefree teenage life thinking about Will, wondering if he's borderline trouble or if he's just a semiregular teenage boy. How do you know when somebody crosses the line? A wiggly line you can't always see?

And to make matters worse, how can I help comparing him to myself? That is, maybe I'm just a Goody Two-shoes, and maybe it's me who should loosen up and get a little crazy once in a while.

Me? Crazy?

Crazy.

Which is a brilliant segue to the one remaining (non-?) member of the Baxter clan.

I'm talking about the chalk line outlining the missing father figure in the family portrait.

A domestic crime scene.

Yellow police tape crisscrosses the sound stage.

Do not enter. By penalty of law.

"Come out with your hands up, William Edward Baxter."

Dad did his vanishing act when Will and I were in preschool.

The story goes that he drowned in a bottle of booze.

Glug.

Then he went up in a haze of pot smoke.

Poof.

And for the grand finale, he disappeared in a cloud of dust.

Snort.

Just like that.

I've been spared all the intimate details, so I've had the good fortune to tap into my own morbid imagination to color between the lines. I get to write my own plotline, to craft my own dialogue, to compose his final scene.

Exit stage left.

Mom never got over it, Dad leaving. In some ways, she still seems trapped under it, like she's forgotten how to breathe.

I remember a few things about him, memories that seem to jump out of the few snapshots I have of him, like the one where he's holding Will on one knee, me on the other, sitting on that brown plaid sofa that's on the back porch now. Sometimes I take the magnifying glass to see if there's something of him I can recognize, anything of him I can see in Will, or maybe in me.

But I can never be sure.

Then I pull back the glass, stretching him out, making him into a freak of nature, a total distortion. Something that can never be repeated.

Or can it?

I try to erase him.

I try to not feel him.

I try to not listen.

Insert sfx: Echo. Slow delay.

Dad.

Dad.

Dad.

Dissolve to oblivion.

Scene 2

Flashback: Family meeting. Around the metal-top kitchen table painted with a green wood grain effect, floral accents on the sides that fold down.

Green wood grain?

Note to self: figure that one out next time.

Let the family meeting commence.

ME: Mom, what exactly are they building at night, in the dark, underground?

MOM: It's just one room, with a set of stairs and a bathroom. A ceiling fan would be nice. It won't be anything fancy. Just the basics.

ME: The basics, as in, a bomb shelter?

MOM: I prefer the term "fallout shelter." Word choice is everything, you know.

WILL: Wow, that's pretty cool. A real live bomb shelter.

MOM: Look, kids, that's not the kind of information you'd want to go spreading around.

ME: How did you think up this one?

MOM: I suppose I have to share some of the credit with Emeril.

ME: Emeril?

MOM: I was imagining a world where everything changes, a world without those everyday experiences that give us structure and stability. The ones that shape who we are, even if they don't seem like much at the time. Like watching *Emeril Live.* It just got me thinking that you can't be too protective these days, now can you?

Huh?

WILL: It's like our very own personal Department of Homeland Security, and you're the head honcho.

MOM *(flattered)*: I hadn't thought of it that way, but I suppose you're right, metaphorically speaking.

Great. Thanks for nothing, Will.

I had to think fast. Say the right thing. Make the right verbal move.

Sure, I'm willing to beg.

ME: Mom, please. Think about it. People don't build those things anymore. Especially in Red Creek. This shouldn't be a dangerous place.

MOM: I just wanted to warn you: there'll be a lot of digging.

Meeting adjourned.

So the very next night, under a high cut of moon, a silhouette of three quiet men broke silent ground on the Baxter family bomb shelter.

Scene 3

"Sky, I want you to record your life."

That's how it started.

A punchy one-liner.

On the *last day of school.*

In the video art studio that doubles as the janitorial supply room.

Throw in a clunky video camera. (Hey, does anybody know they've downsized these things since the Battle of the Bulge?) Toss in a fully rechargeable battery pack. And don't forget the handy-dandy carrying case to boot.

And top it all off with that oh-so-hopeful look on Ms. Assenza's pink dimpled face. Accentuated by those one-of-a-kind earrings made out of bent paperclips.

"Record my life?"

I could see it now: a twenty-minute snippet of Skyler Baxter. My sixteenth summer trapped on celluloid. Nothing held back. Here I am. Look at me. Watch my every move.

Rated G. Approved for general audiences.

Come one, come all. A perfect family flick. A wholesome home video.

Just my luck.

"You're one of our best and brightest," she yodeled. Her excitement sometimes gets the best of her. Makes her lose perspective. She calls it tapping into the cosmic ooze.

With all that enthusiasm, you'd think she was a teenager, not a card-carrying member of the National Association of Teachers-Called-Back-from-Retirement-Because-They-Couldn't-Get-Anybody-Else-to-Teach-the-Class.

"But I'm a photography girl, I don't know anything about video." The ideas floating around my head proceeded to swim the backstroke right out of my mouth.

Ms. Assenza didn't miss a beat. "The basic design concepts from still photography translate quite nicely to video, you'll see, and you have a great eye, don't ever forget it."

Motion sickness.

I was officially outside my comfort zone. It had taken the sum total of two seconds to get the hang of my digital camera, and maybe three seconds more to get the feel for setting up a decent shot. To take some pictures I was proud of. Not bad for somebody who has trouble doing anything that's all that remarkable.

Still life was my specialty. Still is.

And now I was being asked (commanded?) to start firing at moving objects? Moving objects such as myself?

I don't think I'm your girl, Ms. Assenza.

Okay, maybe it's my own flippin' fault. Unlike the kids who want to make something of themselves, I made a commitment to the Visual Art Sequence.

Drawing. Painting. Sculpture. Ceramics.

1-d. 2-d. 3-d. Howdy-doo-d.

All taught by the one and only Ms. Assenza (the only teacher on the planet who still rides a three-speed bike to school).

I took them all. Isn't that enough? Haven't I paid my creativity dues?

I even volunteered to have cafeteria straws stuck up my nostrils while Ms. Assenza poured Plaster of Paris on my face as part of the annual mask-making demonstration.

Not great for achieving that peaches-and-cream complexion.

But a movie of my life?

Overexposure.

I might have to draw the line. It's now or never. Speak up, Skyler Baxter, or forever hold your peace pipe.

"I got a grant. Everything is paid for. Take as many blank tapes as you need," she warbled.

Words stuck to the roof of my mouth. Verbal peanut butter. Extra crunchy.

"I won't know what to do," I told her.

"It's simple," she said, "tell me your story. Listen to your inner dialogue. Discover your passion. Just press play and record at the same time."

Ms. Assenza had some wacky ideas, but this one sure took the Hungarian bundt cake.

For one thing, who'd want to view my life?

For another thing, do I even have a life?

Sometimes I wonder.

But I could use the extra credit.

And my summer job at the Dairy Queen dried up.

Slurp.

Thank Goddess.

And it might be my chance to become a shining star.

Or a black hole, depending on how you look at it.

"Let the lens be a window to your soul," Ms. Assenza said.

Why do I feel like I'm in the confessional booth?

"Bless me, Father, for I have no life."

Then before I could make a graceful exit, she handed me her ostrich-feather pen and the AV equipment clipboard.

"Put your Joanna Hancock right here," she sang.

I looked at her, then watched the purple feather swish around as I signed on the dotted line.

VIDEO DIARY, ENTRY ONE

VIDEO: *Fade up to EXTREME CLOSE-UP of SELF. SELF'S hair is forced back behind camouflage headband, revealing lucky-dice earrings dangling from LARGE PROTUDING EARS. Ugh.*

AUDIO: Dear Diary. Okay, this feels kinda weird, and that's me being honest about it, like it or not. Call me a crummy actress, but I can't pretend that this is one bit fun. For one thing, I belong on the other side of the camera. That's what I'm used to, putting the lens between me and the outside world like some protective shield or force field. And now, here I am, stuck doing a "What I Did on My Summer Vacation" video. Just like those first-day-of-school essays I used to despise when I was a kid. But at least now I get to call the shots. I get to see things and show things the way I want to see them. The way I want them to be. Hey, with the right angles, maybe I'll even add a little excitement to my life. Now that would be called creative genius, that's for sure. It's creepy being on the other side, with me talking like this. Blah. Blah. Blah. So that's all you're getting out of me today, and let's not forget: I'm only doing it because Ms. Assenza wants me to juxtapose a video diary between scenes. So, I surrender. Here I am. And in the end, I can edit out anything that's a little too up close and personal. Anything that doesn't show me as the highly intelligent and fascinating human being that I am. Basically it'll be a seven-minute piece encapsulating the entire summer, exactly what I'm required to do. No more, no less. That's all you're gonna get.

So hello, little metal box. Welcome to my world.

Over and out.

VIDEO: *Fade to black.*

Scene 4

Diagonal wipe: next day.

The Baxter family abode.

I chalk up a lot of my mother's ideas to an overactive imagination. Like getting us to play "Supermarket Sweep" at the Mini-Mart. Or baking birthday cakes in the shape of insects. (What kid wants to eat a boll weevil?) Or wearing her curly red wig to parent-teacher conferences.

"Just jazzing things up, Sky," she's told me time and time again.

I forgot to mention my mom's a writer. One of those creative types. I usually like to leave it at that, but the truth is, she writes romance novels. The ones you find at the supermarket checkout with the guy who looks like Fabio on the cover.

Yes, my mother writes about rippling flesh and pulsing desire and bulging manhoods.

Puh-leeze!

Lucky for me she uses a pen name: Nikki Boudreau. Her editor came up with it. He said it sounds a lot sexier than Barbie Baxter.

Personally, I don't like the sound of "sexier" and "Barbie Baxter" in the same sentence.

And if that isn't bad enough, I get zero sympathy from my best friend, Cat, better known as "Mary Catherine O'Connor" in the permanent records office at Red Creek High.

Conversation in Cat's room:

ME: Why can't she write something normal, like cookbooks or encyclopedias or magazine articles?

CAT: You're lucky your mom is so open about sex.

ME: Yeah, I was the only kindergartner who could label every single part of the entire female reproductive system. Now that's what I call lucky.

CAT: I bet you were princess of the playground.

ME: Sometimes I wish she'd just go away.

I saw the hurt fill Cat's eyes and wished I could pull back the words. Her mom died when she was little. Cat doesn't remember her at all. And no brothers or sisters to share the pain, just Cat.

ME: I don't always feel like that. Just sometimes. She's not that bad, really.

CAT: I know.

I'm the only friend Cat invites to her house. She lives on the outskirts of town, kind of plopped down behind the abandoned Food Lion like one of those green Monopoly houses. Her dad got remarried to Susan, who's pretty strict, never smiles. She's on the night crew at Dunkin' Donuts. Cat's father, like most men in Red Creek, including my dad up until he vaporized, worked at the foundry, but he stopped working five years ago after he hurt his back. Now he calls himself a collector. In the side yard, there's a broken-down car propped up on blocks, a dozen rusty lawnmowers that never get fixed, a refrigerator with the door off so kids won't get trapped inside.

Cat would like to make it better, to clean it all up somehow, but inside and out, her place is filled with stuff too heavy for her to move.

"Mary Catherine, don't you know what time it is?" Susan shouted from the kitchen.

Cat rolled her eyes.

"Visiting hours are over," Cat said.

She needed a diversion.

"Hey, don't worry. Tomorrow night, I'll have a surprise for you," I said.

"You getting your belly button pierced? Your mother will kill you."

"My mother might kill me, but not for that."

"Cat." It was Susan, from the mudroom.

"She's right. It's getting late," I said, making my way to the front door.

"Tomorrow night," Cat called, punctuated by the bang of the screen door as I ran out into the night.

Scene 5

Fast forward: following night.

Glowing from the TV light, Mom had fallen asleep on the couch, holding the remote control to her heart like a prayer book. She reminded me of my glow-in-the-dark Madonna. I flicked off the TV, covered her with the afghan, then switched off the light.

Cat was waiting outside.

"Your time has come," I said, leading Cat down the side of the house, behind the aluminum shed.

The grass was gone where they had made the hole. Just soft overturned dirt remained, no life at all.

The thick metal door to the shelter was flat to the ground, behind a row of hedges. I lifted up the fake Astroturf, a remnant

Mom had found in the garden department at Wal-Mart.

And there it was.

Exposed, the metallic surface was flawless, like a brand-new dime.

"It looks like a little dance floor," Cat said.

"Or a casket," I shot back.

I unlocked the deadbolt, grabbed the handle, and swung open the door.

Nothing but black.

We walked down the wooden stairs, me first, then Cat, her hands on my shoulders. My fingertips read the cinderblock like braille.

I felt for the light switch. *Click.*

"Ohmygawd!" Cat gasped.

"Welcome to the Baxter family bomb shelter."

"It's kind of cheerful in a creepy kind of way," said Cat. "Who did the sponge painting?"

"Take a guess. She wanted to make it more homey, so she

bought a gallon of sunshine yellow and a sea sponge. Some grow lights, too."

"You won't be complaining when you're stuck down here for fifty years, now will you, little missy?" Cat said. I smiled. She did a great Susan imitation.

I felt my smile disappear as I scanned the L-shaped room. Everything seemed squished together, like too many people crammed onto an elevator.

The futon was pushed back against the wall, with the floor-to-ceiling shelving units. A shower curtain swimming with cartoon fish was hung over the shelves, fully stocked with canned goods my mom had arranged in alphabetical order.

Asparagus: upper left.

Yams: lower right.

The generator, a shiny blue metal box, was in the crook of the L.

"Mom says it's our lifeline," I told Cat.

Panning clockwise around the room, I noted bottled water covered with a tarp. A digital wall clock to keep track of our hours underground. Small boxes of dried goods (freeze-dried scrambled eggs with bacon bits, freeze-dried lentil soup, freeze-dried chicken Polynesian, freeze-dried tuna noodle casserole).

Freeze-dried indigestion, anyone?

The boxes were stacked in a perfect Egyptian pyramid on top of the mini-fridge Mom picked up at the neighborhood garage sale.

Under the stairs was a deep freezer next to a bathroom that was so small, you could wash your hands and make a pit stop at the same time.

Note to self: smuggle in ample supply of antibacterial hand wipes.

Next was a pea green metal wardrobe.

Contents:

> Collapsed double-decker army cots (4)
> Flashlights (4)
> Navy blue wool blankets wrapped in
> plastic (4)
> Small pillows, like the ones you get
> on an airplane (4)
> Gas masks (4)

"Check these out," I said, throwing the pillows at Cat, one by one.

"Why four of everything?" Cat asked.

"You know how my mom's in search of Mr. Right."

"You, Will, your mom, and Mel Gibson. How cozy."

I rolled my eyes, and Cat grinned.

On with the panning:

Four doors with brass knobs were in the cabinet below. Cat opened them one by one, pointing to the contents of each compartment, like Vanna White.

"Ladies and gentlemen, this attractive yet practical entertainment center features a selection of the most popular board games. Jeopardy. Risk. Family Feud. Survivor. Providing hours of fun for the entire family who's hiding underground."

I was laughing now.

"And here we have a set of exquisite plastic dinnerware. This service for four includes heavy-duty cutlery, as well as deluxe-size Styrofoam plates (our new octagonal shape) and elegant plastic wineglasses with removable stems for easy cleanup. Perfect for post-catastrophe dining."

"Stop! You're cracking me up!"

She swung open the last door.

"And finally, you—yes, you!—could be the lucky winner of a fine selection of magazines. Take your pick from such explosive titles as *Bomb Shelter Illustrated, Bomb Shelter Weekly,* and *Good Bomb Shelter Keeping."*

"Just the diversion you'll need in the event of the terrorist attack we've all been waiting for," I added in my best game show voice.

We flopped down on the futon and started laughing and hitting each other with those tiny little airplane pillows.

VIDEO DIARY, ENTRY TWO

VIDEO: *Fade up to MEDIUM SHOT of SELF in BEDROOM. SELF is wearing oversized pj's with bacon-and-eggs motif. SELF is sitting on edge of bed with messy bedroom background for realism and convenience.*

AUDIO: So this is my summer to figure out my life, to answer the monumental question, "Who is Skyler Baxter?" Now that's a scary thought. So this video camera is like my very own personal sherpa on what could be a treacherous, high-peaks journey of self-discovery. The extreme sport called ME. "The video camera is your friend." So said Ms. Assenza when she handed me the camera like it was the Hope Diamond. (The Hopeless Diamond is more like it.) She said I should unleash my imagination. Another scary thought. As in, I should imagine the camera to be anything or anybody I want it to be—Johnny Depp is a top choice—and I can talk to it any way I want. This device in front of me is the lens to my internal world. Of course I have to do this project, whether I like it or not, and I swear to you, it's "or not." However, number one: I can't disappoint Ms. Assenza. She's counting on me. And who else in the Video Art Sequence would come through for her? Don't make me list the pathetic nonpossibilities. Number two: I'm the only one who'll see the tape. And number three: I can edit the video any way my little vascular organ desires. A little snipping and splicing can work wonders; it's the nip and tuck of video surgery. Hey, why not? I can do an extreme makeover of my life. And if my instincts are right, I'll be needing to work a few miracles. For now I'll just say that I'm Skyler Baxter. Age sixteen. With no boyfriend and no current prospects present in this time zone or in the entire Western hemisphere for that matter. And I might as well admit to being the only living virgin known to man who's enrolled in the tenth grade at Red Creek High. Oh, except for my best friend, Cat. But don't worry, we're working on it. It's my other summer project.

VIDEO: *horizontal wipe to black.*

Scene 6

Will was looking for us in the backyard when Cat and I came back up a little before midnight. I was realigning the patch of fake grass when I heard his friend Kurt's tires squealing, his radio blasting the hard rock station, as he peeled out of the driveway.

"So what do you think of the underground palace?" Will asked Cat.

"Nice place to visit...," she said.

"...but she wouldn't want to radiate there," I finished.

Will smiled at Cat. He had kind of adopted her like a second sister a long time ago.

Then I noticed his eyes. Puffy. Red. Glazed over.

"Where were you and Kurt?" I asked, suspicious tone in check.

"Nowhere. Just driving around."

I took a freeze-frame of Will, trying for a second to see past my suspicions, to give him the benefit of my doubt. To size him up on a basic fundamental level.

Will. Most people say we don't look much like brother and sister, let alone twins. Will looks taller than he is (five-feet nine) because he's pretty thin in an athletic kind of way.

I call it the Beanpole Effect.

Will's fuzzy reddish hair is always sticking out in at least one spot, so he usually tries to squish it down with an Anaheim Angels baseball cap, then he's out the door.

"Kurt was looking for Michelle," he said, unfreezing my picture of him.

I felt a pull in my chest. I had some kind of feeling about Kurt, even though I wasn't sure what it was.

"Did you find her?" Cat asked.

"Nope, never did," said Will.

I noticed Will's eyes again, but this time they seemed wider, like they were propped open without any toothpicks.

Maybe he was just wound up.

"He thinks she's avoiding him. So he was kind of ticked off. You know Kurt," he said.

Insert sfx: Heavy sigh.

I wish I knew Kurt. A mystery man. I need a secret decoder ring to figure him out.

I noticed my own vocabulary dried up like burnt toast whenever he was around, a fact I'm sure he found incredibly charming and attractive.

"I'd better get going home. Lockdown's at midnight," Cat said.

Will lifted the hatch in the Jeep, folded forward the backseat, and slid Cat's bike inside, then he jumped in the passenger side, with Cat sliding to the middle.

I gave a quick glance up to the Goddess of Four-Wheel Drive Vehicles, thanking her for any influence she just had over making me designated driver. In case Will actually needed one.

Yes. There is a Goddess.

We drove just a few blocks before we hit the main street, Promise Avenue. The Scrub-a-Dub Laundromat. Then the make-your-own-necklace shop: Bead Heaven. At the center of town, the Landmark, an old-fashioned movie theater with red velvet seats and a huge screen that's duct-taped together in the upper-right corner. Next, the new age bookstore, the Enchanted

Spirit, with its crystals and incense and tarot readings on Saturdays.

The sounds of "Achy Breaky Heart" came from the Village Tavern jukebox, then faded as we headed out of town. Me and Cat and Will were big fans of the oldies.

"You ladies going to the bridge tomorrow?" asked Will.

The bridge. Our summer hangout on the Red Creek River, so named because of the clay deposits that color its water (footnote: Ms. Horsington, ninth-grade Earth Science). It was like our own private property until Red Creek Outfitters started renting out inner tubes so out-of-towners (also known as Martians) could ride down the bloodless rapids, whooping it up like they were on the Amazon or something.

"Sounds like a plan," said Cat as we pulled in front of her house. "I'd better get in there. Can't keep the warden waiting."

"Tomorrow," I said.

I watched Cat walk her bike toward the garage, then disappear behind the banged-up trash cans inside the chain-link fence.

Scene 7

"Wanna stop by the diner, score some grub?" said Will while I pulled a U-turn, starting our circle back to town.

I didn't have to answer. He knew I'd take him wherever he wanted to go, and follow him, too, for that matter. No questions asked. A sisterly no-brainer.

"The five-alarm chili's calling my name," he said.

"Well, I'd say you have no apparent choice except to give it a straight answer," I said back, emphasizing the "straight" part.

But the whole thing flew right over his foggy head.

I thought about probing further into his early-evening activities, but I stopped myself. Call it trusting what he'd already told me.

Or honoring a basic respect for his privacy.

Or having a monumental fear of the possible truth.

Ding! Ding! Ding! We've got a winner here!

Maybe it's better to take action. To hope that a little food and conversation might bring him down from anywhere else he might be.

The Last Resort was our after-hours stop-off. I wish I had a nickel for every stale doughnut Will inhaled there.

With all that loot, we'd both be able to retire to Florida. Home of the Early Bird Special. "Get here by 4:00 p.m. and grab all you can eat for just a dolla-ninee-nine."

Will's idea of paradise.

"That stomach of yours, it could win a contest, maybe bring you fame and fortune," I said, trying to keep things light, slipping into my circus sideshow carnie voice. "Step right up. See the man with the incredible gut. He walks, he talks, he ingests large objects like a reptile."

Will laughed. I coasted into a parking spot right in front. We both hopped out. I tried to breathe in. The hot air was thick as motor oil.

"Hey, can I have a little appreciation here? Look what my appetite has done for our social life."

He held open the door and let me go first.

"Don't remind me," I whined.

I gave the place a once-over.

Jack Duncan getting a refill on his cup of joe. Mandy Henry snapping her gum and filing her nails. Mr. Firethorn complaining about his bill.

Same old, same old.

The red-and-white genuine pleather booths with a window view of the parking lot. The scuff-marked checkerboard linoleum floor. The long silver-speckled counter with its worn-out red stools.

Pan countertop.

AUDIO: New age music with James Earl Jones overdub. "With the precision of the Pythagorean theorem, tidy groupings of sugar containers, salt and pepper shakers, ketchup bottles, and hot pink Sweet 'N Low packets decorate the culinary landscape."

Or if you prefer to travel the horror flick route: "Attack of the Killer Flavor Enhancers."

Or a mystery? "The Case of the Missing Tabasco Sauce."

Any way you look at it, this place could definitely use a little spicing up.

"Now this is what I call excitement. Thanks for everything," I said, pointing my voice down to Will's belly.

We took the booth nearest the door. Will shoved a quarter into the miniature jukebox conveniently mounted at the end of our table. Two seconds later, "Help" filled up the room. Will was a huge Beatles fan.

A tear in the seat scratched the back of my leg, so I inched myself over to lean against the steamed-up window.

I stared at Will while he checked out the smudged-up menu that would easily provide the Red Creek Police Department with a complete fingerprint file for almost every member of the local community.

You can never be too careful.

Note to self: make fingerprinting suggestion at next school personal-safety assembly.

I thought more about Will, how we had always hung out together. Inseparable. Like best friends, people said. Unusual for siblings. But lately Will went off on his own a lot. Maybe it was the natural order of things, maybe it wasn't weird or unusual.

"You okay?" I asked. It just slipped out. Fried eggs on a greasy griddle. What was I talking about? How could I back myself up? I had no specifics, zero evidence that something was wrong.

Just this vague feeling that made me want to either throw up or faint.

Second option preferred.

"Why wouldn't I be? You worry too much," he said, reaching over and pushing my shoulder. "Cheer up, Sky."

I sat up, then looked out the window through a fossil of my hair imprinted on the wet glass.

He's right. Will was good at talking me down from my hyperactive mind.

Me = World's Biggest Worrywart Since Forever.

"Congratulations, Skyler Baxter, you get the blue ribbon for self-inflicted mental torture."

That's what you get for inheriting the imagination gene. The worst possible scenario is always just a nerve synapse away.

Stephanie, our favorite night waitress with the biggest hair in Red Creek, sidetracked me from my potential meltdown.

"What can I get you kids?" she asked, wiping crumbs off the table, then putting on her purple half glasses, flipping to a fresh sheet on her little pad.

"I'll have a low-fat bran muffin and half a grapefruit," I said.

"You want fries with that?" Will wisecracked.

"I can't help it if you follow the food abyss instead of the food pyramid," I fired back at him.

"But look what it's done for my fabulous figure," he said.

Stephanie giggled. So did I.

"You twins read each other like two peas in a pod," she said.

Stephanie served up mixed metaphors like she served up mixed vegetables.

All you can handle, and then some.

Stephanie went off on a tangent about the new megastore down the road, how it had its very own restaurant, how every ninety-nine-cent broiled hotdog it sold took away business from the diner, and why didn't it just stick to selling discount clothes and cleaning supplies and winter tires...

Etc.

Etc.

Etc.

I tried to concentrate, but my brain was someplace else, on some distant planet in another galaxy, far, far away. A galaxy called Will Baxter, brother-at-large. I looked at him hard, wondering what questions I should ask, asking myself if it was time for the first degree.

Will placed his order, his voice echoing like it was bouncing against the walls of a deep canyon right before someone falls in headfirst, out of control, never coming back.

Scene 8

By the time we left, Will seemed more himself, so I handed him the keys when he asked for them.

We headed back down Promise Avenue.

"I told Kurt I'd stop by," Will said.

"Tonight? Mom doesn't even know we took the car. And we were supposed to be home by dark. Do you really want to get her all crazy?"

"Don't worry. I've got it covered," he said, looking at me with that smile of his.

Will was born with an overdose of charm. He draws people to him like sugar ants to a bowl of Cap'n Crunch.

But sometimes I think Will gets himself into situations on purpose, knowing how "that smile of his" can unglue him from the stickiest kind of mess.

And getting into trouble gives him some kind of electric charge, a heart-thumping thrill. It's like he's invented this emotional roller-coaster ride where he's planted himself in the front seat of the very first car. And it's a really fun ride.

Wheeeeeeeeee!!!!!!!

Meanwhile, I'm standing on the ground, watching him through the hand over my eyes, a meat grinder churning the most recent contents of my stomach.

Before I could finish the laundry list with every reason why Will should call it a night, we were back home.

"What if you get pulled over?" I blurted out. "You don't have your night license yet."

Not bad for a last-ditch effort, I thought.

"You'll be my one call, you can come bail me out," he said, smiling. "You'll sacrifice your babysitting money for me, won't you?

I gave him an unsteady smile.

Sometimes I wish I could open up a faucet and let all my worry leak out.

Drip. Drip. Drip. Beware: hazardous waste site.

But it isn't so simple when the worry includes Will.

I can't turn it off when it comes to him. No matter how hard I try.

Sometimes when I see Will, I see a stand-in for Dad, a kindred understudy. A shadow waiting in the wings. A confidante. A protector. For me and for Mom, too.

Sometimes when I see Will, I see an experimental film starring my father. Separate reels of film, spliced together, in no particular order. No shot list, no continuity.

The image is blurred.

Who is the father?

Who is the son?

Sometimes when I see Will, I see the chances Dad took, the high stakes he played.

A roll of the dice.

Snake eyes.

Sorry, sir, you lose everything.

As in, yourself.

As in, your family.

P.S.: your kids lose everything, too.

As in, you.

Just like Dad, Will likes playing dangerous games.

Go directly to jail. Do not pass go. Do not collect $200.

But what can I do? Lay down the law? Make a citizen's arrest?

William Baxter Jr.: You've been charged with breaking and entering your twin sister's comfort zone. Anything you say can and will be used against you.

Will snapped me out of my funk when he clicked off the headlights. He turned down the radio and eased the car into neutral as we creeped in front of the house, then came to a silent stop. Mom was a light sleeper, so we had our little bag of tricks to make sure she didn't wake up.

As I grabbed the door handle, Will's voice drew me back like a giant magnet.

"Did Mom tell you about the guy she met?" Will said.

Insert sfx: skidding tires.

"Don't tell me. I don't want to know. Who is it this week?"

"Some guy named Ed. He's stopping by tomorrow. 'To meet the kids,' she said."

"Not again."

Ed. Rhymes with: dead, lead, dread, butthead.

I felt my shoulders fall forward, so my chest looked even more caved in than it usually does.

"Hey, who knows. Maybe this guy is different."

"You're starting to sound like her." My voice, a flat line.

"Cheer up, Sky. We can get past it."

"Why are we always getting past stuff? Why can't we just stay like we are?"

"Mom deserves a little happiness, some companionship, dontcha think, little sister?"

If Will is the Fiji Islands, I am Siberia.

Is anybody sure one of us wasn't switched at birth? It must be confusing at the hospital, keeping track of twins.

I shouldered open the door, then gave Will the "are you sure you want to do this?" look, but all he did was smile (see what I mean about that smile?). I jumped out of the car, and off he went.

I saw the taillights flash on, slicing blood red across the yellow newspaper box as he turned the corner and drove out of sight.

Then I stood there with this empty feeling, wondering why Mom always wanted more, why it seemed Will and I were never quite enough.

Scene 9

I couldn't feel my body once it hit the water, the life flash-frozen right out of me, like chicken nuggets in a TV dinner. I felt myself getting sucked all the way to the bottom, my feet stomping the feathery weeds, pushing off on the smooth, slimy rocks, then springing me up to the surface.

The water in the Red Creek River didn't warm up until August. We were still getting winter run-off that started way up in the high peaks, where the snow lasted until the end of May, sometimes the beginning of June.

"Hey, Cat! Your turn!" I called out, shading my eyes with my right hand as I looked up, treading water with my left. Then I swam back to shore.

Cat stood on the lower deck of the bridge, one of those erector-set types, about as high as a three-story house that seems like the Eiffel Tower when you're way up there looking down. She faced out, but her arms were pushed back, wrapped around one of the crossbeams. Her toes peeked out over the edge.

"Cowabunga!" she yelled, jumping off, wiggling side to side in her California surfer pose.

I laughed, even though that was probably the ten millionth time she'd done that.

I held my breath as the dark red water swallowed Cat up, and I didn't start breathing until I saw it spit her out again. She took three strokes to get back to shore, then slipped out of the water and sat next to me.

"There's Will," she said, looking toward the dirt path we'd engraved at the side of the woods.

"Hey," I called out. Behind him came Kurt. I felt my breathing pick up. Then behind Kurt came Michelle.

I turned away, a sting in my chest.

"Why did they have to bring her?" Cat growled, noticing the look on my face. She didn't miss a drumbeat when it came to me.

"Can't blame him," I said, trying my hardest to believe it. "What healthy, all-American boy doesn't love arm candy?"

"Too much sugar rots the teeth, in my humble opinion, and in the opinion of the American Dental Association," she said back.

I liked the authority in her voice.

Will and Kurt climbed up the bridge to the lower ledge. They let go straightaway, doing Tarzan screams at the top of their lungs, then they were silenced by the water, first Will, then Kurt.

Michelle stood away from us, her arms crossed and right knee bent, looking like she was waiting to catch a bus to the mall. Her strawberry-blonde hair was in an updo. She wore white platform sandals that tied around her ankles, a watermelon-colored tube top, and cutoff shorts. The sun caught her face and set off that sparkly junk girls like to smear all over themselves. And the whole package was topped off with cherry red lip gloss.

Oh-so-very-kissable.

I snapped my gaze from Michelle, over to Cat, then out over the water, like advancing frames on a 3-D Viewmaster. *Click. Click. Click.*

I looked down at my pathetic self. I was wearing the same old ratty blue-striped bathing suit I've had since ninth grade. The kind that hangs on you like elephant skin.

Then there was the prickly stubble sprouting on my legs like genetically engineered crabgrass.

Hey—anybody got a spare Weed Whacker?

Michelle was everything I never was and never could be.

I tried to use my fingers as a comb for my hair, which as usual was a barbed-wire mess. I could never get that one right. What can you do you if your hair's as curly as a miniature poodle's? Stick one of those cutesy little bows at the top of your head like you just spent the morning at "Yip 'n' Clip" groomers?

Bowwow.

Will and Kurt slid up on the grass and sat on the other side of Cat.

Kurt's summer skin was the color of graham crackers, the cinnamon sugar variety (my personal favorite), and his brown hair made me think of dark chocolate.

Imaginary pickup line, showing my playful side: "Kurt, pretend I'm a marshmallow, and let's make a human S'more."

Kurt pulled a comb out of his back pocket, ran it through his curls, the tips letting go steady drops of water.

Imaginary pickup line, showing my sexually enlightened side: "Kurt, did you know that erotic sensations travel from skin to brain at 156 miles per hour?"

He glanced back at Michelle.

"Gotta go," he said, standing up.

Imaginary pickup line, showing my desperate side: "Aren't you forgetting something, as in, 'me'?"

"Already?" asked Will, disappointment in his voice.

"You know, the ball and chain."

I felt Cat fire a look at me, but I stayed looking straight.

"Be right back," Will said to us, then he followed Kurt over to Michelle.

"I don't get it," Cat grumbled.

She lay back on the grass, looking up at the clouds like they were spelling out some kind of an answer.

Cumulus smoke signals.

I watched Kurt grab Michelle's hand, then disappear into the woods.

Would I ever not inhabit the land of Eternal Geekdom?

I climbed to the top of the bridge, and when I reached it, I held tight to the hot metal, then let go of myself, closing my eyes and falling slow motion into the blackest part of the river.

Scene 10

If my dating history was a stale soda cracker, my mother's was a big hunk of triple-decker death-by-chocolate cake with double-fudge frosting, extra thick.

The first bite tastes sweet, but two swallows later you're searching for the nearest vomitorium.

A Dating Game spin on things:

Bachelor number one: Lenny, professional bowler.

"He's hit 300…twice! And he's correcting my hook!" Mom beamed.

One month later, Lenny went on tour, never to return. Wrist guard and all.

Bachelor number two: Dr. "Just-Call-Me-Pete," family dentist.

"He adores my bite!" she gleamed, clicking her choppers like a set of wind-up plastic teeth.

Within three weeks, Mom found out that Dr. "Just-Call-Me-Pete" also adored his dental hygienist, with whom he was having a love child in the spring.

Bachelor number three: Harvey, podiatrist.

"He says I have a perfect arch!" Mom sparkled.

The very next day, Harvey's size-thirteens walked him straight back to his ex-wife.

So you can imagine my excitement over meeting Ed. And—lucky day!—Mom was on her way to pick him up right now.

Knock. Knock. "Sky?"

Will opened my door just a crack.

"I'm afraid so," I said.

I was lying facedown, pillow over my head, my arms and legs all stretched out like a flattened mosquito.

Splat.

"Why don't you give the guy a chance?" Will said. The bed sank and the springs squeaked when he sat down next to me.

Will is an integer.

I am a negative number.

I pushed the pillow off my head (which was really needing some air right about then) and sat up to face him.

"It's called logic, using your brain, learning from your mistakes. When the same problems keep cropping up over and over again, when every one of the guys Mom meets is a loser, well then you put it together and know that this one will probably be a loser, too. Loser plus loser equals loser. Why doesn't Mom get it?"

"Okay, okay. Just because she paints this rosy picture, you can't blame her for that."

"The rosy picture that always includes her going into her bedroom and not coming out for three weeks once she finds out that her Ed is really an Edwina or something?"

We heard Mom's signature "Shave and a Haircut" toot—her sunny way of saying, "Kids, I'm home! And I've brought my little Ed with me! Today's man of my dreams!"

Will stood up and looked at me with his sad eyes. My heart felt weighted down, like it was made of raw cookie dough.

"Sometimes I just don't get you, Sky."

He turned and walked off, shutting the door behind him.

Most times I just don't get this family, I mumbled to myself.

Then I heard Mom set down grocery bags on the table and sing from the kitchen: "Kids, come meet my surprise!"

My cue.

I flopped back down on the bed and smushed the pillow over my head.

VIDEO DIARY, ENTRY THREE

VIDEO: *Hard cut to SELF lying on back. SELF is holding camera in right hand, pointing at SELF. CAMERA TECHNIQUE: shaky cam. TRANSLATION: too lazy to set up tripod.*

AUDIO: For once I don't mind talking. So, okay, Señorita Camera, you're not a someBODY, but at least I have someTHING to talk to. At this point, I'll take whatever I can get. Why doesn't Mom get it? I am not the least bit interested in meeting her latest Romeo. I could be doing a million things more productive than that. Like picking out the sock lint that's lodged between my toes. Anything where I'd have something to show for it. Great. Someone's coming to dig me out of my grave. Or to drop me deeper into it. Thanks for listening. Adios.

VIDEO: *Press POWER OFF button. BLACK SCREEN.*

Scene 11

Tap. Tap. Tap.

If only it were killer termites. Or mutant carpenter ants. Or radioactive roaches. But, no, it had to be Mom.

"Sky, I insist that you come out of your room this instant," her impatient whisper forced its way through the keyhole.

I played dead.

"I'm waiting, Sky."

I played deader.

"Okay, then. I want you out here the second the Minute Rice is done."

Clack, clack, clack. Her sensible shoes walked back to the pot of rice.

I rolled over, got myself up, and looked at the train wreck of me in the full-length mirror on the back of my door.

Down again.

Time for a little self-talk: Okay, Sky, sit up straight. Put on your orange-slice smile. Fix your tumbleweed hair. Very good!

Now create a mental checklist of this evening's coping mechanisms:

- ✓ In my head: recite Gettysburg Address in Pig Latin
- ✓ Play invisible game of tic-tac-toe on ceiling tiles
- ✓ Count my toe hairs
- ✓ Have out-of-body experience where I time travel to another dimension

Repeat positive affirmation: you will get through this night.

I will get through this night.

I will get through this night.

I will get through this night.

Scene 12

Will was sitting at the kitchen table under the plastic cat clock with the swinging tail and the rolling eyes that seemed to be checking us out.

Tick-tock. Tick-tock.

A domestic time bomb.

Mom was flitting around the kitchen making dinner. She was all hopped up, like she was being jolted by an electric current running through the linoleum.

The back of a head was staring at me. I imagined drawing a smiley face on the baldy spot with my scented Magic Markers.

Have a nice day!

"Sky, we're so glad you could join us," my mother said, a chirping bird.

I didn't say, "I'm so glad I didn't have a choice in the matter."

I did say, "Uh-huh."

"Sky, I'd like you to meet Mr. Dickey."

I felt my left eyebrow go up like it was being pulled by a string.

I didn't crack up and say, "Mr. Dickey?! Hey, newsflash! Doesn't anybody see a possible problem here?"

I did smile and say, "Hello, Mr. Dickey."

Mental math problem: romance writer Nikki Boudreau + Stud Muffin Ed Dickey = Romance Writer Nikki Dickey.

Mr. Dickey half stood up and reached out his hand to me.

His fingers felt like cold hot dogs.

"Please, call me Ed."

I caught a whiff of his aftershave.

Eau de Bug Spray.

He wore brown plastic glasses, the kind with the automatic shading feature (smoky gray), so it was hard to make out his eyes. He was wearing a polyester golf shirt (blue paisley) and khakis (tan) with perfect creases running down the legs.

No laugh lines or worry lines creased his clean-shaven face.

Yes, Mr. Dickey appeared to be a wrinkle-free man.

He noticed me looking at his gold belt buckle with the letters END on it.

"Stands for Edward Nicholas Dickey," he said.

Thought bubble: is anyone into symbolism here?

"Your mom is a special lady," he said, looking at Mom with bassett hound eyes.

Mom smiled back at him, then she peeked under the lid to the rice pot.

Please, Lord, let it be the steam that's making her blush.

She turned on the oven light, peeping through that little window at an avocado green casserole dish. When she turned to face us, the red oven mitts on her hands looked like boxing gloves aimed right at me.

She was wearing her tie-dyed jumper and brown sandals. Circles of beaded bracelets (made by hers truly, of course) were clinking around her wrists. Her curly reddish-blonde hair, pulled up into a scrunchie, looked like flames shooting from her head. Her hot pink lipstick went a little out of the lines around her mouth.

Seeing her there like that, trying so hard, I felt a twinge in my heart.

Then I glanced around the kitchen.

A bottle of uncorked champagne stood on the table next to two crystal glasses etched with the date of her marriage to Dad.

How could she?

A plate stacked with Italian wedding cookies sat waiting on the countertop.

"What's for dinner?" asked Will, self-appointed Chairman of Chow.

Why can't I be the one who's oblivious?

"It's Taiwanese Anniversary Chicken," she said, sticking a big spoon into the Crock-Pot and stirring twice.

I didn't say, "What are you waiting for, Mom? Why not wear your wedding dress to dinner?"

I did say, "Sounds delicious."

Will shot me a look that said, "Show me a little sincerity here."

"Everything looks lovely," said Ed, squeezing my mother's hand.

She pulled out the casserole dish and set it on the seashell hot plate in front of him, next to a basket filled with tortilla chips.

"It's smoked oyster dip," she said, scooping some dip onto a chip, then offering it up to Ed, like she was serving him Holy Communion.

Instead of grabbing it with his fingers, he reached forward and sucked it all straight into his slimy mouth.

Insert sfx: toilet plunger.

Looking up at my mother, he said with Bambi eyes, "Did you know oysters are considered an aphrodisiac?"

I pictured myself picking up the champagne cork and popping it directly into Mr. Dickey's mouth, trapping the smoked oyster dip inside there until the end of time.

And we were only on the appetizers.

How would I ever survive the main meal?

Scene 13

"So, Sky, I understand you've inherited your mother's writing talents," Ed commented, then he took a big gulp of the foamy red drink that Mom had pureed in the blender.

The little paper parasol sticking out of it almost went up his left nostril. When he set down the glass, he had a cherry mustache.

Tee-hee.

"I keep a journal, that's all," I said.

"Ed's creative, too," my mother injected like a verbal syringe.

"Oh, yeah?" asked Will, conversationalist extraordinaire.

"Yes, he designs computer systems, don't you Ed?" my mother said. "He works out of his finished basement."

"That's how we met, through the computer," Ed said. "In Chill 'n' Chat."

"Chill 'n' Chat?" I asked. My voice was as flat as my so-called chest.

"Yes, Chill 'n' Chat," said my mother. "It's an Internet chat room where parents can discuss their special problems."

"Special problems?" I asked.

"Yes, special problems that come with raising teenagers," she said.

"As in, special problems that come with raising Will and me?"

Run-on sentence ricocheting inside my head: "As in, special problems about raising teenagers that's really about Will and me that you're discussing with complete and total strangers such as Mr. Dickey, who's sitting at our kitchen table wolfing down our Taiwanese Anniversary Chicken like there's no tomorrow?"

Insert spfx: my head spinning around, Exorcist *style.*

"No need to get defensive, dear," she explained, pointing her fork at me, then plinking it down on her plate. "Problems with teenagers are as old as the hills. Aren't they Ed?"

"Well, I suppose so. But I can only speak for my cats."

His cats?

"I have no real children myself. Well, I guess my cats are my kids. Ike and Tina are twelve months old, that's sixteen in human years."

"Imagine that: they're the exact same age as you two kids," Mom said. "And a boy and a girl, too."

Will and I looked at each other. If this was a cartoon, our eyes would be popping out of their sockets on springs. *Boing! Boing! Boing!*

"The cats were getting a little rebellious, so I decided to seek a little expert advice from barbie_doll," he said.

"Mom, please tell me, not barbie_doll," I heard myself whine.

"It's a perfectly legitimate screen name, right, meow_man?" she purred.

Meow_man?

"Before you knew it, barbie_doll was my own personal 'Dear Abby' for cats. It's always plain to see who's a genuine cat person."

I can see her new bumper sticker now: I ♥ ED'S CATS.

"But Mom, you're completely allergic to anything with hair," said Will.

No need to worry about Ed in that department, I thought.

"Yeah, remember how you blow up like a balloon and you get those red bumps all over yourself if you come anywhere near cats?" I chimed in.

Subtext: Can't you see how Ed is all wrong for you? Don't you know you can do better than this?

Mom fired us both a look that said, "Don't wreck this Kodak moment."

"I'm perfectly fine if I remember to take my antihistamine," she said.

"I can't imagine how I ever lived without her," Ed announced.

"Don't let him fool you, kids," Mom giggled, slipping her hand over his.

When she said it, I felt a spidery chill crawl up my back and down my arms.

Something about meow_man gave me the major creeps.

It was Mom and Ed on one side of the vast frozen tundra, with Will and me on the other. At this point, Mom would need a major sledgehammer to break the ice.

Mom took a swing.

"Ed, why don't you share something with the kids about your cats?"

Okay, Ed. Here's your chance to redeem yourself. Show us your stuff.

"I'm a firm believer in the value of leading a disciplined life. My cats are on a strict schedule from sunup to sundown, including an exercise regimen and a mandatory nap schedule," Ed said, showing off like he was up for a part on Animal Planet.

"Mandatory nap schedule?" I said. "Isn't that a little hard to pull off?"

"Not when you have a good alarm clock and a decent crate system," he bragged. "I even count out their kibble."

"You count the cat food? Every single piece?" asked Will, looking sideways at me.

"Piece by piece—125 per cat per day. We don't want to spoil the little creatures now, do we?" he said, looking over at my mother for her *Good Housekeeping* seal of approval. "Not to mention those unwanted calories."

Say something, Mom. Kick Ed off his soapbox. Tell him he's nuts. Show him the way out. Say farewell, Ed! For now and forever!

But noooooooooo.

Ed opened up his big trap one more time.

"A little self-discipline never hurt anyone. Spare the rod, spoil the child," he said, looking smack-dab at Will. "Not that I advocate corporal punishment—in most cases, that is."

I wondered what Mom had told Ed, what family secrets she'd let out. How she might have bailed on Will, and maybe on me, too.

"If only they could talk, I'm sure they'd thank you for it," Mom said, sliding her chair a little closer to Ed's.

Ed smiled at my mom as he grabbed the pink cookie shaped like a leaf that sat on top of the three-tier dessert tray.

"What a perfect evening," Ed said, pink crumbs sticking to his lips like some weird tropical fungus.

My gulp of milk suddenly clogged up my throat like Elmer's Glue, so I coughed it onto my napkin.

Hey! Does anyone happen to notice I'm choking to death here?

Insert sp fx: a big fat pencil eraser comes down through the ceiling, rubbing out any trace of this entire night.

Scene 14

"Congratulations. Sounds like you passed the Barbie's-New-Boyfriend-Torture-Test," Cat said, kicking back on the bomb shelter futon, chugging back a can of root beer.

"Just barely. You wouldn't believe how sugary sweet they were to each other. It's like eating a roomful of cotton candy. Makes me want to gag."

I flopped down next to her. She offered me a sip, and I took a big swallow, then another. Bubbles burned the back of my throat, making my eyes water.

"But there's something about Ed Dickey. Something rotten, I mean."

I reached down and turned on the radio. The oldies station. "Nowhere to Run" was playing.

"Well, at least your mom has someplace to direct her attention," she said.

"And while she's distracted, we should decorate this place. Spruce it up. Add our own personal touch."

"You'd better hope your mom's mind is completely on Ed and completely off you," Cat said. "Otherwise you're completely dead when she finds out. She doesn't ever want you down here, let alone me."

"I'm being considerate. It's all her stuff. Let the decorating begin."

I had already lugged down a cardboard box from the attic.

"Check this out," I said.

I lifted out a lava lamp with dull orange globs settled like sludge on the bottom.

"Now this is very cool," said Cat, taking it to the power strip and plugging it in. She set it on top of the microwave. The yellowish light woke up the globs and they started mutating.

Upset stomach under glass.

I pulled out a long strand of red chili-pepper lights that Mom liked to string under the patio umbrella when we had summer picnics. "And these whimsical details will lend a festive flair to your most important occasions," I said in my interior decorator voice.

"Those'll look great running down the stairs," said Cat, plugging them in, then twisting them around the wooden handrail.

"And let's not forget the love beads," I said, yanking them out of the box.

"Most groovy, baby," Cat said, making a peace sign.

After we hung them from the beam at the base of the stairs, we took turns walking like movie stars through the iridescent strands, the plastic beads clinking together like tiny bells.

"And this is the best of all," I said, lifting out the globe that looked like the giant fly's eye in the biology room.

"The disco ball!" we screamed out together.

I ran over to the boom box and loaded my mother's "Dynamite Disco" CD, punching in selection 7.

The intro to "I Will Survive" blared out of the speakers. While I hopped up on a chair to hang the ball, Cat entertained me by mouthing the words to the song and acting it out, using the empty root beer can for her microphone.

At the end of the song, Cat gave a bow, then plugged in the cord to the disco ball and clicked off the overhead light.

The next disco selection: "Stayin' Alive."

I did a couple of my John Travolta moves that only Cat would appreciate. She jumped onto the chair and shined a flashlight down over me like a spotlight.

We both flopped down on the floor, giggling away.

Cat and I knew each other so well we could fill in each other's blanks. Sometimes I wondered what it would be like if I found a guy who could understand me that way.

But for now, it was just me and Cat, looking up, hypnotized by the sound of the Bee Gees and the sight of the disco ball that was sprinkling millions of tiny little stars all around the room and over us both.

Scene 15

"What are you guys doing down there?" we heard Will yell.

"Nothing. Come down and find out," I said, sitting up, fixing my ponytail.

I heard Will's footsteps first, then another's.

Kurt.

My heart. *Ta-dump. Ta-dump. Ta-dump.*

"I thought maybe you kidnapped the Bee Gees and were holding them hostage," Will said.

Then he made a weird haunted-house laugh.

Will came over to me and put his face next to mine.

"What's the matter, Sky?"

"You smell funny," I said, scrunching up my nose, pushing him away.

I looked over at Kurt. His eyes looked like blue marbles stuck in mud.

"What have you guys been doing?" I said, my voice unsteady. Like it was playing on an old cassette tape.

"Just hanging out," said Will.

"You've been partying," Cat said.

"I can smell beer all over you," I said.

"What are you Inspector Gadget?" Will said, holding up his arms like he was under arrest.

Kurt made this sloppy half-smile.

"Come on girls, loosen up a little," said Will. "Don't be so serious."

Kurt came closer to me and propped himself up against the entertainment center. His eyes stayed on me for a few seconds.

It felt like the very first time he had ever really noticed me, a pink feather duster feeling in my stomach.

Thoughts about all the oh-so-clever things I would never be oh-so-clever-enough to say spun inside my brain like sweat socks in a dryer.

Someone clean out the mental lint trap, please.

I snapped out of it when Will reached in his pocket and opened up his hand like an oyster. And inside the oyster was a half-smoked joint.

Dad.

"Will, what are you doing?" I said, my voice low.

"Well, I know what you're doing: you're turning into the vice squad," he sneered.

My eyes stung. I turned my head away.

And with the flick of a Bic, he lit it up.

Will took a hit, holding it in, then letting it out, sending up a thick smoke screen all around him.

"It's no big deal, just a little relaxation," said Will, passing the joint to Kurt.

I watched the end of the joint burn orange while Kurt held it to his lips.

Cut to fried egg.

Voice-over: This is your brain. This is your brain on drugs.

Sssssssssssssssssssssssssssssss.

"You girls want some?" Kurt asked.

It felt like the room was running out of air.

"We have to go," I said, turning to Cat. My out. "I'm driving Cat home."

Cat underlined my words: "I gotta get back."

Kurt slid down to sit on the floor against the wall. He took a dark brown bottle out of his pocket. I heard a quick sizzle when he twisted off the top, then flipped it at Will.

Kurt and Will laughed.

Cat and I didn't.

"You girls look like you're at somebody's funeral or something," said Will.

I wondered if he was right, if something between us was dying, if it was already dead.

Cat started up the stairs, and I followed. I stopped on the second step, using the railing to hold me up, looking back at Will through the waterfall of love beads.

I saw him take another hit, smoke filling up all the space that was left between him and me.

I turned away and escaped up the stairs.

Scene 16

On my way home from dropping off Cat, the night seemed too dark and quiet, like something right out of *Scream,* just before somebody gets decapitated or otherwise knocked off.

I looked up through the windshield at the lights in the sky, wondering if all of them were stars.

There has to be at least one spaceship up there.

Maybe I'll be abducted by aliens who'll suck out my brain and replace it with spinach.

I should be so lucky.

Cat had tried to give me a pep talk in the car. She told me not to worry, that lots of kids are into partying, that Will is going to be all right, that he is really okay right now, and that I really need to get a hobby, a hobby that isn't Will, exclamation point!

I nodded my head yes, yes, yes, as she told me all that, but inside myself all I was hearing was no, no, no.

Driving back home through town, Promise Avenue looked like a fake Hollywood set, like the fronts of the buildings had nothing at all behind them except wooden studs propping them up.

No life-forms anywhere in sight.

What if I suddenly stopped breathing? Who would be around to call an ambulance, to give me mouth-to-mouth, to administer last rites? This place was totally unprepared for a possible state of emergency.

Note to self: send letter to the editor re: lack of adequate authority figures in town.

As I turned off toward our house, I was praying for a giant billboard displaying step-by-step instructions about exactly how I should feel, precisely what I should do:

SKYLER BAXTER
CALL NOW FOR ANSWERS
DIAL 1-800-GT-A-CLUE

But instead all I saw was a sign for the Red Creek Body Shop:

YOU BLOW IT, WE TOW IT

I noticed that Mom's bedroom light was on when I pulled into the driveway.

I dropped my keys on the kitchen table, *cha-chunk,* and went down the hall to her room. Her door was opened just a slice.

"Mom?"

"Come on in, Sky."

She was sitting at her computer. I plopped down on her bed, which was covered with a leopard-print comforter to match the jungle theme in her room. It looked like Cheetah could swing down from a vine any second now.

"I have a deadline next week. It's been hard to get anything done. I've been so distracted lately."

Too distracted because of Ed Dickey? Too distracted because of Ed Dickey to see that your own son is being sucked into the sewer? Too distracted because of Ed Dickey to see that if Will is sucked into the sewer, he'll be living with all the alligators people flush down their toilets, if you don't get totally un-distracted right this very minute?

"Sky, I feel I can be frank with you. I'm worried about Will. That he may be heading down the same dark path as your father," Mom said.

She looked helpless, sad, vulnerable, in a way I never knew before.

"Tell me I shouldn't worry," she said.

Wait a second. Who was I to make things better, to come up with the magical solution? I am so not qualified.

Before I could come back at her, she went on. Spilled more of her guts.

"I didn't know how to handle your father, so how can I possibly fix things with Will? It all seems beyond my capacity."

I didn't say anything. Still.

It felt like she was letting it all hang out to dry. But the wet heap of her emotions was falling straight on top of me.

Umph.

"Some people suggest vitamins or yoga or biofeedback therapy. I'd be willing to try just about anything, what do you think?" she said.

But she didn't give me a chance to answer.

"Forget I asked. I hate to put you in the middle of it," she said. "You've never given me any trouble."

Me, the good girl. Why did I always have to be measured in comparison to Will? And when I came out ahead, why did that feel so cruddy?

The computer screen backlit her head like a halo.

She looked at me over the red polka-dot half-glasses that were resting on the end of her nose, the multicolored beaded chain strung around her neck. Gray strands of her hair seemed for the first time more obvious than her strawberry blonde. The thin lines on her face, like cracks in glass, seemed permanent and deep.

I felt a press on my heart, thinking she looked older than I remembered.

"What was Dad like?"

A shadow of sadness fell over her face. There was always this silent undertow pulling on her, on us all, like she had never really gotten over him, like she still missed him somehow, even after everything he put us through. Even though he left a long time ago, he was still around in some big quiet way.

"Never mind," I said. "Forget I asked. I don't know why I did."

Nothing like dropping the A-bomb on your very own mother. I felt like telling her to run for cover. All because of me.

I turned away, moved toward the door.

"You thinking of him lately?" she asked.

I turned back around.

"Not too much," I said. "Sometimes, a little, I guess."

She looked to the side. Talked to dead air.

"Drugs and booze, they did him in," she said. "Our lives could have been so different."

I just stood there, listening to the same old story, still wondering what it would be like if it were different. Better, I mean.

She looked up at me, gave me that no-nonsense look.

"Never forget, it's in the genes," said Mom, her voice sounding like a prerecorded message.

How can I forget? You remind me every chance you get. *Reefer Madness. Girl, Interrupted. The Days of Wine and Roses.* You made us watch it twice.

My father: the gateway drug to our inevitable downfall.

Forget I asked.

Regroup.

"But what was he really like? I mean really. Him."

Press pause. Now play.

Mom took off her glasses, strung them over the edge of her computer screen.

"Your father was a good man who loved you very much," she said, her voice soft and sure.

I waited. Don't let it end here. Tell me more. I want to know everything. Anything I could never find out for myself.

Please. Don't make me beg.

"He was a sculptor. That's why he worked at the foundry."

I knew all that, I'd heard it a hundred times, but I felt like I needed to hear it again, like maybe there was something I'd missed, like maybe it might seem different this time.

Mom continued.

"Of course, he was much too talented to work there. They never utilized his gifts. Whenever he could, he loved working with a slab of clay or a block of wood, finding things hidden inside. That was when he was truly happy. If only we lived in Paris. They really appreciate artists in France. They even have their pictures printed on the money. Can you imagine that?"

Thanks for the crash course in world currencies, Mom.

Let's turn the camera back on Dad. Where it belongs. Distant, but in focus. At least for the time being.

Dad.

As I thought it, before I said it, my brain had a sudden flash of Will. About his mysterious ways lately. About the funny feeling I had in my gut when I thought about him, about what he might be up to. Or not.

"What about Will? Are there any good ways he reminds you of Dad?"

"Well, they're both outgoing and fun. Everyone loved Dad, always wanted to be around him."

"What about me?"

Insert long, painful silence.

"You have his caring side, the side that takes things hard and seriously. Everything was always about him, even when it wasn't. He made it like that, in a good way. If you know what I mean."

For once I knew exactly what she meant.

"And that's the side of him I loved the most."

I leaned over and gave her a kiss, the first one in I don't know how long.

She had a question mark on her face as I closed the door behind me.

VIDEO DIARY, ENTRY FOUR

VIDEO: *Checkerboard dissolve to CLOSE-UP of SELF. SELF's hair has been dyed PINK due to previous evening's spontaneous splurge with a box of strawberry JELL-O.*

EDITING NOTE: *Cut angles that accentuate pink drip line on forehead.*

AUDIO: Let me get to the point. Why can't Cat be a boy? Then maybe finally I'd have a chance to date someone that (a) I like, and (b) likes me back. Not to mention that we might be able to have a normal conversation, where every little thought isn't all jammed up inside me, which always happens whenever I want to talk to a boy I like—as in, Kurt. It's like I'm brand-new to the English lan-guage. Like I have no idea how to construct a simple sentence. Like I couldn't conjugate a verb if my life depended on it. Maybe if I ever get the one fat chance of being with Kurt, I'll just try to picture Cat's head on top of his shoulders. Then the real me will come out, the one that I actually like. Hey, a little creativity never hurt any-body. Except maybe Jack the Ripper. Or the Unabomber. Or Martha Stewart.

Gotta go live the life so I might have a little something of impor-tance to say that is somehow at least loosely connected to reality.

VIDEO: *Checkerboard DISSOLVE to BLACK.*

Scene 17

The heat woke me up early the next morning, pushing down on me like a giant steam iron.

Whooooooosh.

My windows might as well have been painted shut. No air was coming through the screens, and none was getting out.

I wished one of those airplane oxygen masks would drop down from the ceiling. Anything to help me breathe easy for once.

Fat chance.

My throat tightened up. *Cough.*

Get me out of here.

I forced myself out of my room, slinking down the hallway to Will's room.

He was up to something. Exactly what, I wasn't quite sure. But I was ready to find out.

Insert sfx: Mission Impossible *theme builds in background.*

On his door was a fluorescent orange sign with big black letters:

POSTED:
VIOLATORS WILL BE APPREHENDED
AND PROSECUTED
TO THE FULLEST EXTENT OF THE LAW

Be careful what you wish for, Will Baxter Jr.

I hadn't heard him come back the night before. Not that I would. He's pretty stealthy when it comes to reentering the homestead in the wee hours.

I nudged open the door, then held my breath and stepped inside.

His Milky Way galaxy bedsheets were all in a heap, making it look like maybe he was deep in there somewhere, lost in space.

But when I pulled them back, nothing was there, like I'd just performed a vanishing act.

Abracadabra!

Insert sfx: audience gasps.

Where is Will?

The question sucker punched my gut.

Whomp.

More jabs followed.

What is Will up to?

Jab.

Why do I have this creepy feeling?

Jab.

What is it that I don't want to know?

Knockout.

When I came to, I knew my next move. The bomb shelter. Sometimes Will headed down there to avoid the possibility of being busted by Mom for breaking curfew.

I updated my itinerary.

New destination: underground.

Scene 18

When I got there, no Will.

But signs of him were everywhere, anywhere.

I sat on the futon and scoped out the room.

Used-up tissues like fallen angels on the floor. Half-empty glass of watered-down Coke. Ripped-open box of saltine crackers, a trail of crumbs sprinkled across the carpet. Dirty clothes in various random locations.

And top it all off with that inescapable funky odor.

Marinated sweat socks.

Pewie Louie.

But hey, isn't this typical for a teenage boy? Wouldn't it be strange if it were somehow otherwise?

Possibly. But I need to find out what's going on, if anything.

If.

That's when I decided to start the formal investigation.

As in, snooping around, like any decent, well-meaning too-nosy-for-her-own-good sister would do.

I'd like to say a little birdie told me to do it, but that would be a lie. I did it all by my yellow-bellied sapsucker self. Yup. The same self that is too chicken to ask the right questions, to confront Will directly.

With a *cluck-cluck* here, and a *cluck-cluck* there.

I zoomed in on the framed picture standing on the center shelf in the entertainment center. It was of me and Will on the *Maid of the Mist* at Niagara Falls. We were wearing those blue hooded raincoats, smiling from earlobe to earlobe, like we were the happiest kids on planet Earth. Like we had no idea that someday I'd be on the verge of busting my very own brother.

But that was then. This is now.

You need to face the facts. Only, you have to find them first.

But where?

The bomb shelter offered limited availability in the "Favorite Places to Stash Stuff" department.

Where to start?

The metal wardrobe.

It felt like some giant magnet was pulling me to it.

I did not resist.

I surrender. Take me to your leader.

I stood there facing it, then unhooked the latch, swung open the doors.

Voila!

An overflowing blue plastic laundry basket was crammed inside, alongside a beat-up Frisbee and a deflated basketball. Not to mention the cracked baseball bat, the falling-apart catcher's mitt. Looked like Will was using the wardrobe for his own personal gym locker.

I went for it.

My hands fished through the unopened package of tightie whities, the wrinkled black boxers covered with multicolored pool balls, the wide selection of rolled-up tube socks and crumpled up T-shirts representing Will's most memorable concert experiences.

It was like being stuck inside a clothes dryer. No order. Everything tossed around without a care in the world.

I dug in deeper, aimed for something, anything, underneath it all.

Please.

Let there be nothing here.

Show me that Will is okay. I mean, really okay.

Let me know that I don't have to worry. That everything's cool.

Give me a sign.

That's when I found it. A round metal container. The kind those stale butter cookies come in.

Pulled it out.

Flipped the lid.

There it was. Buried treasure.

Five little packets of white powder.

Holy shitaki mushroom!

Weed is one thing. But coke? Or heroin? Or Goddess knows whatever else this stuff might be?

My heart dive-bombed to the floor.

Welcome to the Big Leagues, Will.

But that wasn't all.

Shining up at me was my great-grandfather's gold pocket watch. My great-grandfather's pocket watch that was given to me. My great-grandfather's pocket watch that was given to me, not Will.

Liar. Cheat. Thief.

Perpetrator: Will.

Victim: your very own sister.

How could you?

I leaned against the wardrobe so I wouldn't fall over.

This was wrong. All wrong.

Without thinking, I dropped the watch down my shirt. Lucky for me it fell inside my AA bra. Who would ever think to look for it there?

I felt like I was stealing my own property.

Which I was.

Wasn't I?

Before I could wrap my cranium around it all, I heard the door open. Somebody at the top of the stairs. Somebody whistling a happy tune.

Will.

Abort.

I buried the evidence, silently pushed in the wardrobe doors, then looked up, too stunned to know what to do next.

Scene 19

Somehow I managed to scramble to the futon, scoot on top of it, pretending to read the copy of *Rolling Stone* I snagged from the floor at the very last nanosecond.

Talk about a hair-trigger reaction. One of the few benefits of being a total nervous wreck.

Will stopped dead in his size twelves when he saw me. Stood there with this tough-guy look on his face, like he was posing for a mug shot.

Smile!

"Hey," he said, acting cool.

"Hey," I said back, acting cooler.

I need more time. Time to think. Time to plan my strategy. I am dealing with someone I used to have a handle on, someone I used to know.

But not anymore.

Out with the old rules. In with the new.

"What's up?" he said, his words oozing thick with suspicion.

I wanted to say: I'll tell you what's up. *You* are up. Up Shit Creek, that is.

But instead I said: "I was looking for you. Where've you been?"

A diversion disguised as a seemingly innocent question. I didn't want it to seem weird that I was in the bomb shelter. Get the scent off the trail. Lead Will across the river, like good cowboys do when they're trying to lose the bad guys.

I'm a real sucker for Westerns.

"Just hanging out."

He threw down his backpack on the futon right next to me. Like a challenge. Just try it. I dare you to look inside.

"Sorry to cut the party short, but I need to crash for a while," he said.

I stood up. He lay down. Covered his eyes with his bent arm.

Rope him in. Pull it tight. Don't let him get away.

I need to say something. After all, this is my brother. Not some strange, demented pervert lurking in a dark alley.

What am I so afraid of?

"Will."

He looked at me. Now was my time to speak.

"I'm worried. About you. About what you're up to. You don't seem like yourself lately," I said, hearing the warble in my voice.

It was a start. Not great. Better than nothing.

"I don't know what you're talking about," he said, his voice edgy, defensive. "Don't you have better things to think about than me?"

He turned toward the wall, as far as he could get away from me.

Dead end.

"Will."

No answer.

Maybe I should pull the goods out of the wardrobe. Show him

the watch. Demand an explanation. Lay it all out in front of him. Literally.

Or maybe not.

Be honest.

I am not prepared to accept that Will is not who I thought he was.

I am not prepared to believe that Will is turning into Dad.

I am not prepared to figure out how Mom fits into all of this.

In fact, I am not prepared to pretend I know what to do at all.

But.

I am prepared to bolt. To tell myself I'll deal with this later.

To be a coward.

To turn my back. To walk away.

Which is exactly what I do.

Insert sfx: door slamming shut.

Scene 20

Meanwhile, back at the raised ranch.

Ed Dickey was fast becoming a permanent fixture at the Baxter family dinner table.

He'd plopped himself at the dining room table every night for the past two weeks at 5:30 sharp, looking like some tacky candelabra that no one would buy if it was the last garage-sale item on Earth.

Not only that, he took it upon himself to claim the head of the table as his very own.

I want to ask, who gave you squatter's rights?

I want to ask, who appointed you CEO?

I want to ask, don't you have someplace else to go? As in, someplace that isn't here?

But instead I just sit there like a lump of cold rutabagas.

While Will sits there as high as a Chinese box kite.

Hey, doesn't anybody hear the ticking time bomb? See its sizzling fuse all lit up like a Fourth of July sparkler? Isn't it time to throw some water on it? Call in the bomb squad? Shouldn't we close our eyes, cover up our ears, hit the dirt, alert the neighbors in the event of an explosion?

Shouldn't somebody cry, "Help"?

Naw. We're too busy partaking in ethnic cuisine with a worldly flair.

Priorities.

Mom got into a thematic cooking routine, thanks to the spreadsheet Ed Dickey so kindly produced and stuck on the refrigerator with four kitty-cat magnets.

> Mondays ~ Mexican
> Tuesdays ~ Japanese
> Wednesdays ~ Italian
> Thursdays ~ Chinese
> Fridays ~ Indian
> Saturdays ~ Middle Eastern
> Sundays ~ A smorgasbord of the
> finest international leftovers

And you guessed it: Mom dressed accordingly. And she played music straight from the "Country-of-the-Day" on her turntable from the 1970s.

Shouldn't someone commit that thing to the Smithsonian? Pronto?

"There's nothing wrong with doing our part to advance multiculturalism in Red Creek," she said, puffing her words through the chartreuse veil over her mouth, cascading over her belly-dancing outfit. "Acceptance of differences begins in the home."

I skimmed the room's present occupants. Mom. Will. Ed Dickey. Me. A roomful of difference, that's for sure. Sorry, you'll have to take a number, one new difference at a time.

I felt my mouth drop open, but no words came out.

Then Mom's *I Dream of Jeannie* slippers jingle-jangled back out into the kitchen, en route to replenishing the babaganoosh.

Will sat there watching the steam curl up from the plate of spinach squares. I could swear the smoke spelled out "SOS."

Save Our Selves.

Then Ed Dickey had to add his three cents.

"Your mother's right. It's like starting our very own United Nations," Ed claimed like he was presenting his closing argument on Court TV.

"Or our own little global disaster," I mumbled to Will.

"Or our own little World War Three," Will mumbled back.

Will and I started that kind of giggle that gets worse the more you try to stifle it.

Ed stopped his forkful of Lebanese tabouli midflight.

"Why don't you two let me in on your little joke?" he snarled through a fake smile.

Ed was like a pressure cooker, ready to blow its lid.

Ka-blooey!

Will was stone faced, staring straight ahead.

If this was the mess hall, suddenly Ed Dickey had promoted himself to drill sergeant. And Will and I were his new recruits.

"Get it together, you two," he ordered, his voice deepening two octaves. "Or else."

Gulp.

Then Mom glided back into the room.

"Kitten, set down that bowl right next to me," he said, all nicey-nice.

Where did the real Ed Dickey go? And who's the imposter taking his place?

Mom took her place right next to you-know-who, patting his super-sized dimpled hand that reminded me of a catcher's mitt.

"Look at us all, my dream come true," she warbled.

Q & A for my mother: don't you know a nightmare when it's staring you right in the face?

There was nothing stopping Barbie Baxter when she entered her Dreamworld. It wouldn't matter what Will or I or the president of NOW would say.

I wanted to change everything, to press reverse, to go back to the way things were before. Pre-Ed Dickey.

I wanted to make everything all different than it really was.

Mission Impossible.

I picked up the bottle of hot sauce and dumped it all over my meal.

VIDEO DIARY, ENTRY FIVE

VIDEO: *FLIP-FLOP TRANSITION to LONG SHOT of SELF standing next to oversized Scooby-Doo plush toy won at Wack-a-Mole booth, State Fair, freshman summer. SELF is wearing vintage El-ton John T-shirt, red plaid shorts, and brown suede moccasins that might be cut off from the frame but are worth mentioning.*

AUDIO: *BACKGROUND MUSIC: Green Day—"Jesus of Suburbia":* Today I stand before you to reveal my innermost thoughts. Which is mainly because my bed is too messy to sit on. Can I let something out that's made a mental traffic jam inside my head? Something that has nothing and everything to do with Will? Okay, I'll just say it. Sometimes I wonder where my father is, if he's anywhere at all. And I wonder if he were here, could he kick some butt with Will? Do the father thing? And while he's at it, why couldn't he take over my worrying part? Maybe make things better. Maybe draw from his own personal dysfunctional experience.

SELF reaches over, presses PAUSE BUTTON.

Video opens to new angle. SELF is lying on PINK SHAG RUG in BEDROOM.

Get real. Will won't talk about him. Doesn't even like to hear his name. He says he wouldn't meet up with him even if he had the chance. I don't know about me. I wonder what it would be like to see him face-to-face, up close and personal. Call it curiosity. Or stupidity. Wanting to get together with someone who could've been the most important man in my life, if only he'd had the guts to stick around. So instead he's a bunch of blank pages in my emotional family album. But say I could talk to him now, with or without Will. Maybe I would find out something about myself, like why I'm the only one in the family who likes old black-and-white movies and why I eat garbanzo beans, straight from the can. You kind of wonder about the who-what-where-when-how-why that makes you who you are. Who doesn't? It's digging to the root of the good old nature-nurture controversy. I wonder what he'd think of me now, if he'd be proud of how I turned out. As if he had anything to do with it. Maybe he'd regret leaving me in the first place. I wonder if he's thought of me at all. Maybe on Christmas or my birthday, if he even cares to remember. That's the least he could do. But since that's an unlikely scenario, maybe I could send him this video of my life, so he could get to know me, the way I want to be known. I could splice my life together, just the good parts, and leave the other stuff on the cutting-room floor.

If only it worked that way in real life.

VIDEO: *SLOW DISSOLVE to BLACK.*

Scene 21

My red Converse high-tops jumped out of the Jeep with me inside them.

I surveyed Cat's house.

The peeling red paint like sunburned skin. The maple tree with a split-off branch hanging down like a broken arm. The storm-cellar doors swung open like a punched-in mouth with swollen lips.

Everything at Cat's seemed to require immediate medical attention. I stepped up to the screen door.

"Hello?" I called.

No answer.

I pushed open the door. Invited myself in.

The calmness of the house startled me. None of the usual tension you need a machete to cut.

I moved through the living room, stopped in the kitchen.

Mismatched dishes with chipped edges piled in the sink. The faucet: *drip, drip, drip.*

Ripped-open envelopes (overdue bills?) scattered across the countertop.

Three chairs turned away haphazardly from the metal kitchen table that Susan had piled up with empty Dunkin' Donuts boxes she was using to store vitamins and prescription bottles and bottles of nail polish.

It looked like everyone had just left in a hurry, each in a separate direction.

The stale cigarette smell made me want to open the windows, turn on the ceiling fan.

How does Cat come up for air? How does she manage to breathe?

I slipped down the narrow hallway, then stood outside her bedroom door.

I tapped twice. "Cat?"

"Hey, you," she said, all cheerful. "You have my permission to enter the chamber."

I pushed open the door, sniffing Downy's baby-soft freshness in the air. There Cat stood, laying perfect stacks of clothes into a pine dresser that we painted all funky-like with Simon and Garfunkel lyrics scrawled over the drawers.

"I am a rock, I am an island."

"And a rock feels no pain."

"And an island never cries."

"You have a real knack for folding, missy," I said. "If I didn't know better, I'd say you have a promising career ahead of you at your friendly neighborhood Gap."

Cat giggled.

"Yeah, pretty sad, isn't it?" she said. "I'm a disgrace to teenagers everywhere."

"Don't give up yet," I said. "You still have potential to turn into a complete slob. It's easy. Look."

I picked up her Bubble Yum T-shirt, balled it up, threw it on the floor.

"Now, repeat after me," I said.

She picked up a pair of cutoff khakis, looking at me with doubtful eyes.

"Let go of all toxic tidiness, young lady, let it go," I chanted.

She threw them over her head, the legs helicoptering down to the floor.

"Brilliant, just brilliant," I said. "Maurice, can we get an instant replay on that one?"

Cat's laughter filled up the room, and somehow it got inside me, too, making me forget everything that was completely all wrong, anything that just wasn't right.

"Susan's on the warpath," said Cat, looking down.

"What for?" I said.

"Who knows. She mainly takes it out on my dad. It makes it hard to sleep, listening to her rage."

I looked around her room, all neat and perfect. You could bounce a dime off her Teenage Mutant Ninja Turtles quilt that she'd had since we were little kids.

Cat's room, the eye of this hurricane house.

"How about you quit the folding marathon, and we go to the bridge," I said.

"Thank you for saving my sorry self," said Cat.

She tossed the plastic hot pink clothes basket on her bed, and it tumbled to the side, clothes spilling out like they couldn't care less, as we darted out the door.

Scene 22

Cat and I watched some Martians float down the river on multi-colored inner tubes underneath our dangling legs. They were bumping and spinning around like giant Froot Loops bobbing around my cereal bowl.

"Remember: buns up in the white water," Cat yelled down to a bald guy with a beer gut floating on the blueberry one.

He flipped her off.

"You have a nice day, mister," Cat shouted to him in her cheery flight attendant voice.

Rocks in the Red Creek River are sometimes hard to see, especially in the rapids, and they can be dangerous, especially to somebody who isn't familiar with its waters. You can never count on anything for certain.

Things shift around unexpectedly. What's safe one minute is unsure the next.

Cat let go a day lily from the bridge. It fell as soft as an orange feather, then floated away like a dead body facedown on the water.

Made me think of Will. Shiver. I crossed my arms tight around my waist and pulled them in.

"You okay?" Cat asked me.

"Couldn't be better. Let's see. Will's getting high on a daily basis, my mother's in love with a computer weirdo, and Kurt finds me about as exciting as poached egg on toast."

"I like poached egg on toast."

"You're the only one. Don't you see, Cat?"

Her upbeat look vanished, like I'd just removed it with a squeegee.

"Sometimes I wish I knew how everything will turn out, that I could fast-forward this tape until the good part," I said.

"What day is it?" Cat said.

"Saturday."

"Your wish is about to come true."

I was too bummed out to demand details.

We pulled on our shirts and shorts all sticky over our wet bathing suits, and I followed Cat down to the path.

As we walked through the woods, I felt a flutter in my stomach at the thought of any wish of mine that might ever come true.

Scene 23

A string of rusty chimes clinked against the glass door, eliminating any chance of our secret squirrel entrance into the Enchanted Spirit.

We stopped to speed-read the bulletin board. Yoga classes. Drum circle. Regression therapy. Reiki for pets.

Reiki for pets?

New age music floated through beat-up black speakers perched like pulpits in opposite corners of the room. Other tourist attractions: Low-back sofa with faded floral cushions that dipped down in the butt region. Helpy-selfy herbal tea bar. Babbling tabletop fountains.

Made me wonder where the restroom is.

Book sections at front: Alternative health and healing. Astral projection. Astrology. Feng shui.

We drifted toward the back.

Body, mind, and spirit. Healing dances. Sound therapy. Witchcraft.

On top of a display case with giant crystals was a cone of incense burning in a clam shell.

Hand-written sign: "Today's Scent—Sensual Seduction."

I took two quick whiffs. Then a slow, deep inhale.

A copy of *The Kama Sutra for Starters* was propped next to it. The cover had two people all tangled up in each other, looking just like a Boy Scout knot.

A rolling double half-hitch, if I ever saw one.

Another sign: "Ignite your sexual fires. Buy both today. Only $19.99!"

Cat and I traded smiles.

A ponytailed college guy with a nose ring, wearing a tie-dyed shirt, was behind the register.

"Ask him for a book review," I whispered to Cat, and she laughed until she snorted.

"Or how about a copy of the movie?" said Cat.

"Or how about a personal, in-home demonstration?"

"Hey—can I show you girls anything?" offered Mister Tie-Dye/Nose Ring/Ponytail College Guy.

Cat turned away and made another snort.

Emergency message to self: divert thoughts immediately to cure acute case of giggles.

Athlete's foot. Can of sardines. Flat tire. Ryan Seacrest.

"No, well yes, we were wondering about the tarot readings," Cat managed to spit out, "for her."

"Yeah, Cassandra's here today. Go on back. She's behind the hand-held massagers."

The loudest Cat snort.

"Thanks," she said.

Cat hooked her arm inside mine and yanked me and her snorting self to the back of the store.

Scene 24

I stopped Cat before she knocked on the door with the purple curlicue lettering:

~ *Your Psychic Passageway to the World of Knowing* ~

Whoa, Nelly.

My feet all of a sudden felt like they were stuck in a tub of edible Play-Doh.

What if she tells me something I don't expect, something I don't want to know?

Cat noticed the monster-movie-matinee look on my face.

She reads me like I have subtitles.

"Don't worry, it's on me," said Cat, whipping out her Hello Kitty wallet.

I did a mental eye-roll.

I should tell Cat it's not the money, I should tell her I'm afraid.

Call me Kentucky Fried Chicken, Extra Crispy.

It's Cat, for gawd's sake. She'll understand.

The door pushed open.

My time was up.

"I had a feeling someone was out here," said a chirpy round lady wearing those chunky plastic glasses from the eighties. Her eyes looked like pool balls through the pink tint. She wore a Hawaiian muumuu and flat burlap sneakers. Her white hair was piled up on her head like a scoop of instant mashed potatoes.

"I'm Cassandra," she said, putting out her hand to Cat, then me.

Cassandra? Maybe Dorothy or Henrietta. But Cassandra?

I tried to not look at Cat.

"Come on in," she sang like an advertising jingle.

She shut the door, then stubbed out a cigarette in a flipped-over peanut butter lid.

"Not to worry, it's herbal. Red Clover. My only vice."

I felt like we were playing mental freeze tag.

Cat and I were frozen stiff, and Cassandra was "It."

"Now what can I do for you girls today?"

"I'd like to buy a reading for my friend," Cat said.

Yikes. Lemme outa here.

"What is it you want to know?" Cassandra said, her bug eyes trained on me.

"Nothing, really," I said.

Now ain't that the truth?

"She wants to know about the past, the present, and maybe throw in a little future," said Cat, my new official spokesperson. "And we only have ten bucks," she added, my new personal financial adviser.

"I suggest a three-fates spread," Cassandra said. "It will reveal significant chakras and energies, and I'll have you out of here in ten minutes."

Cassandra, can you reveal this significant energy: what is Cat getting me into?

Scene 25

"Please," said Cassandra, waving me to the folding chair at the other side of the card table covered by an Indian print cloth the color of Skittles.

I lowered myself down to the very front edge of the chair.

One inch northward and my tushie is flat on the floor.

"Shuffle these," directed Cassandra, "and think about whatever it is, whoever it is, you want to know more about."

She slid toward me the oversized cards, upside-down, their wavy-gravy pattern making me dizzy.

It felt like the room was getting dark, or maybe it was only the oxygen to my brain getting cut off.

I picked up the cards, closed my eyes, and started to shuffle with my fidgety fingers.

"Think of anything you want to know, my dear, clear your mind of everything else," echoed Cassandra's fortune teller voice.

Emergency alert to self: Do not think of Will. Do not think of Will. Do not think of Will.

The more I tried not to, the more I thought of Will.

Can anyone find the off switch for my brain?

After three shuffles, I opened my eyes, then tapped the cards to even the deck. I pushed it between us.

My heart was beating as if xylophone mallets were striking my rib cage.

"Let's start with the top left card, the most important element of the past," said Cassandra..

She turned it over.

Insert sfx: blood-curdling scream.

"The ace of wands," she said. "Clouded joy, some delays. This card evokes a need for patience."

I hear you. I can deal with that. I'm in no hurry to go downhill fast.

"Now the center card, revealing a deciding element of the present," Cassandra said, flipping it face up.

A guy looking up, about to walk off a cliff, a white dog nipping at his feet.

That boy is going down!

"Ah. The fool reversed," Cassandra said.

"What's that one supposed to mean?" asked Cat.

"It represents danger, carelessness, wanderlust. Perhaps obsession with someone or something, strong impulses and desires."

My throat felt like a kinked garden hose. Could Will stop what he was into? Or was he in too deep? I had enough information. Time to say good-bye. Exit stage left. I turned toward the door.

"The right card is a critical element of the future," said Cassandra, and before I could put my hand over hers to stop it, her fingers seemed to levitate the card and flip it over in thin air, right before our very eyes.

Riding a white horse was a black knight holding a black flag with a cross.

"What's that?" Cat asked, her voice a nervous whisper.

"The death card."

I leaned closer, a mealy moth to a Bunsen burner. Fry city.

Inside the armor was a skeleton.

Every arm hair I owned stood up like brush bristles.

"It represents a foolish decision, even a dangerous one. But that choice, however painful, will lead to transformation, a major rebirth."

I already waited for Will to be born once. And it almost killed me the first time. How can I survive it again?

"Here's my advice: don't let what you're seeing blind you to the obvious."

Before she could say another word, I shot out of the room and away from the Enchanted Spirit, those rusty door chimes calling after me.

Scene 26

A little dose of terror set a brush fire under my butt.

I ran like never before.

I needed my fuzzy blue slippers. My "Save the Whales" mug filled with my warm Sleepytime Tea and a spoonful of honey. I needed my Mom's vintage record collection and my beat-up turntable. I needed myself all alone in my house, all wrapped up inside my cocoon bedroom.

Just three driveways to go.

Insert sfx: screeching brakes from a jack-knifing eighteen-wheeler.

My high-tops would not budge, like they'd jumped smack-dab into a pile of ABC gum.

It can't be.

Yes, it is.

The Ed Dickey mobile.

His reconditioned Ford Pinto, dill-pickle green, parked directly over the Texas-shaped grease spot in the middle of our driveway.

I got close enough to read his bumper sticker: "CAUTION! I break for CATS!"

CAUTION! I DON'T brake for COMPUTER GEEKS!

I slithered around the side of the house to the back, where I pulled the lounge chair against the aluminum siding, stood on its frayed woven seat, then pushed open my window screen. I hoisted myself up, up, in, Charlie's Angels–style.

Then I fell on my head, *clunk*, on the hardwoods.

Ouch. That didn't tickle.

I sat on the floor, rubbing my head.

Then I started hearing voices: Mom and Ed.

I took off my Converse, slid them under the bed. I skated on my socks to my bedroom door, my left ear magnifying their conversation.

"Barbie, you must put your foot down, mark your territory, draw a line in the sand."

Huh?

"You're right, of course, it's just that it's been hard without a father figure. Maybe it's been easier on Sky, but Will, he needs someone to look up to, a man who can stand his ground, who knows what he wants."

Easier on me?

"I'll talk to him myself," Ed said, his voice too strict, too much in charge.

"No, it's not your problem. I don't want to drag you into this."

"Any kid of yours who puts his fist through the wall, then takes off leaving you all upset, well that's what I call my business," he said.

Puts his first through the wall?

"I don't know, Ed, I'm so worried. He didn't look right."

"Don't you worry. For now, just leave it to me. And remember, there's always the police."

The police?

I felt like busting in, setting him straight, telling him to back off, we can take care of ourselves, handle our own problems.

A lot of good that would do. Then I'd be added to Ed's hit list.

So instead I hooked the scratchy brass lock on my doorknob, then dove back in my bed, headfirst under the covers.

Scene 27

When my undercover air supply ran out, I wormed my way back out.

It was mid-afternoon already. Time was a-wastin'. I needed to find Will.

I did my Charlie's Angels entrance in reverse, minus the falling on my head part.

Where was he?

My stomach did a belly-whopper.

Coming around the back of the house, I noticed the Astroturf covering the bomb shelter door was pushed aside.

My Will radar started blipping.

Periscope up.

I rotated a full 360 degrees.

The coast was clear.

I yanked up the door and climbed partway down.

"Will?" The blackness swallowed my voice like a giant mouth.

Silence.

I flipped on the light switch, then pulled the door shut above me.

My feet felt unsteady, like they were trapped on those crazy shifting fun-house stairs.

Only minus the fun.

Halfway down the stairs, I surveyed the room. A dark lump of something was on the futon.

Will.

"Will?"

The lump started to morph.

Still no reply.

I took the steps, one by one, until none were left to keep me from what I didn't want to see.

"Will?" A little louder.

Still nothing.

He was all curled up like a jellyroll.

I pushed myself to him, then put my hand on his shoulder.

"Will." Hearing the sadness in my voice, just saying his name, made my heart murky, dark.

He turned over, his arms bent, his hands over his eyes, forming a perfect isosceles triangle.

A geometric tragedy.

"Will." My jigsaw voice in a million pieces.

"Hey, Sky," he said, a smile cutting his face.

I wanted to ask him Who? What? Where? When? Why?

The five essential Ws of solid investigative reporting.

But I just sat there instead.

"Sky, I need some water."

I considered taking one of the spring water bottles from under the tarp but stopped myself. What if Mom finds out it's missing?

I can hear her now, clipboard in hand, pencil propped behind her ear, her Lee Press On Nail poking a graphic calculator: "My supply spreadsheet clearly indicates one missing water bottle. It might not seem like much now, but in a crisis, it could mean the difference between life and death."

And what about Will? How about his life-and-death spreadsheet? The one with black checkmarks filling up the death column?

Will's survival had become my own.

I went over and grabbed a bottle for Will, another for myself, then I chugged mine down while Will did the same.

When Will fell back asleep, I took off up the stairs.

VIDEO DIARY, ENTRY SIX

VIDEO: *Fade up with BULL'S-EYE EFFECT from CENTER to MEDIUM SHOT of SELF, filming SELF in REFLECTION of MIRROR. SELF is ALONE. SELF appears LOST. SELF appears HELPLESS. SELF appears READY TO JUMP OUT OF SKIN.*

AUDIO: What's the one true story about Will? Is he just your average partier or a hard-core druggie? Sometimes I think he's basically not that different from lots of kids who get into some bad stuff on a temporary basis. It's not like it's never been done before. Hello! Flashback to the seventies, for example! And it's not like they don't come out of it, back to normal, business as usual. Case in point: former hippie turned corporate executive. But how do you know when bad is good enough? Sometimes it's hard to see the line, to know when you've crossed over into a drug-induced Dangerland, to realize that it isn't just about fun anymore. When it's more than just a phase. When it's about dependency and getting hooked and having no way out.

Which is Will.

Believe it. It's true.

I don't want to lose him. I already lost my father.

Isn't that enough?

VIDEO: *INVERTED BULL'S-EYE EFFECT to BLACK.*

Scene 28

Cat looked at me through her front door screen, its frayed corners covered with tape to keep the bugs out.

I felt like a visitor talking to a prisoner, a wire mesh sifting the air between us.

"Where'd you disappear to, Houdini?" she said. It was the first time I'd seen her since the Enchanted Spirit fiasco two days ago that seemed like an eternity ago.

"Sorry for the vanishing act, but I had to escape," I said.

"If I had a couple more bucks, I would've asked Cassandra to locate you in her crystal ball earrings."

I didn't have the energy to laugh.

Cat swung open the door, *squeak, slam,* then we sat down together on the porch floor, facing each other.

She assessed the total wreck of me.

"What's wrong?" Cat asked, her voice softer, her eyes clear and wide.

"It's Will."

"What now?"

I broke down and told her everything, my heart letting go of the pressure, like flipping the pop top on a shook-up can of Mountain Dew.

Ed trashing Will...Will trashing himself...

"I don't know what to do," I said, my voice sounding like it had a bad connection.

My concentration cracked like stepped-on ice when I heard Cat's dad and stepmom yelling at each other inside.

Their buzz saw voices seemed to slice Cat in two.

She turned away.

Right then I wanted to ask Cat what was up with her, to tell her I care for her the same way she cares about me.

But my mind circled back to Will instead.

"What should I do?"

"You need to level with him. Tell him what he needs to know," Cat said.

"I need to know it first."

"Just remember, you're his sister. It's up to you to set him straight."

The truth of Cat's words was clear as invisible tape.

I gave her a hug, then took off, heading as fast as I could toward home.

Scene 29

I lowered myself back into the bomb shelter.

Almost dinnertime, and Will was still passed out.

"Will, you gotta get up," I said, pushing him around like I was kneading dough. "We have to talk."

His hair looked like silly string. His pancake face had raisin eyes.

I shut my eyelids to blot out the image.

"What's up, baby sister?" he said.

"Look, Will, I heard Ed talking to Mom. I know about the wall."

He started to get up. I noticed he'd wrapped an Ace bandage around his right hand. Probably from the first-aid kit.

"Man, I gotta go set Ed straight. That asshole really pissed me off."

"No, Will, forget about Ed. Just hold on, sit down, so we can talk."

He crumpled back down on the futon, like a wadded-up piece of college-ruled paper.

"Will, what are you getting yourself into?"

"It's nothing. Stop playing Nancy Drew," said Will, his sharp words giving me a mental paper cut.

I thought about Will and me, how we could always talk, how there was a not-so-long-ago time when we trusted each other.

I had to bring him back, perform the emotional Heimlich maneuver, clear out the blockage so he could breathe again.

"Will, it's me, you can tell me anything, remember that about me, about us?"

I could feel myself drawing a crayon smile on my face.

Will's silence filled the room like mustard gas.

Then he pulled himself up and over to the mini-fridge, and I followed. He opened the door with his bandaged hand. On the shelf were little squares covered in foil, shining back at us like tiny silver jewels.

"What's that?" I asked him, keeping my voice steady.

"It's what you said you wanted to know."

My mouth went dry. I needed water.

If I challenged him, asked too many questions, he'd lock me out, throw away the key.

But I had to find out.

"Tell me what it is," I said.

"Angel dust. PCP. That's all."

My stomach took a nosedive.

I searched my mental files back to the drug unit from health class, but drew a blank. PCP? Angel dust? Why hadn't I paid attention instead of staring out the window, thinking "None of this will ever apply to me"?

"Don't get so freaked out about it," he said. "It's just for fun, no big deal. It's not like I'm doing it every day or anything."

The hostility in Will's voice was something I wasn't used to, something that dive-bombed me, blasted me out of the way.

I stepped back.

What now?

"Just for fun? I don't call this fun." Too late. I was crying now.

Will put his arm around my shoulder, pulled me in.

"You worry too much. I know what I'm doing."

I forced myself to believe it because I couldn't handle the alternative.

"Just be careful, okay?" was all I said.

"You know me."

A rush of cold air hit me as he grabbed a packet, then shut the refrigerator door.

Scene 30

"I've got to pick up the Jeep," said Will. "I left it at Kurt's house to throw Ed off my trail. You in?"

My left kneecap started vibrating.

Was it the thought of Will driving? Of Ed Dickey finding Will? Of Ed Dickey calling the cops?

Or was it the mere mention of Kurt?

Then my right kneecap joined in the fun.

Who knows what's next?

And what happened to that little silver packet?

"You can stay home, Sky," he said, giving me the perfect out.

But I took the revolving door right back in.

"I can go. Maybe I should."

"Forget doing your good deed for the day. You quit Girl Scouts in fifth grade, remember?"

Onmyhonoriwilltrytoservegodandmycountrytohelppeopleat alltimesandtolivebythegirlscoutlaw.

Now *that* memory showed up totally uninvited.

"For your information, mister, those two merit badges are mine for life."

Will smiled, taking off my worry like a wool sweater.

"Three, if you add one for single-handedly devouring an entire box of Caramel Delites," he wisecracked.

He almost looked like himself again.

I threw Will's baseball cap at him. He plopped it on top of his curls.

"Let's go," I said.

"Suit yourself."

We killed the lights and headed up the stairs, first Will, then me.

When we stepped outside, I took in a long, cool breath, then let it out slowly.

"I wonder if Mom considered the fact we'd be breathing each other's air down there," I said.

"Imagine doing that while we wait for the radiation to settle."

"A mere fifty years, give or take."

"If Ed joins us, we're pitching in for an air purifier," Will said.

I smiled.

That's when I thought, maybe things aren't quite as bad as they seem.

That's when I should have thought, don't I wish.

Scene 31

It was getting dark.

Will and I maneuvered down a backyard obstacle course to get to Kurt's.

If we were still little, if things were like they used to be, we'd be playing hide-and-seek, we'd be running through every sprinkler, we'd be climbing, swinging, jumping every chance we got.

We'd be covered with grass stains and our stomachs would be cramped up from all that laughing.

But now everything is different.

Except for one basic fact: Will still leads the way, with me tagging behind.

Kurt was sitting on the front step when we got to his house, his white T-shirt hugging him in all the right places.

I am Silly Putty, you are the Sunday comics. Let me flatten myself on you while you transfer onto me.

No wonder Kurt sees me as invisible.

And then there's Michelle.

I pictured her inside Kurt's Dutch colonial, preparing her fresh-squeezed lemonade or reapplying her Maybelline or sewing her wedding-ring quilt.

Michelle is flaming cherries jubilee.

I am a stale Twinkie.

Will went over to Kurt while I stayed back, propped in the driveway like a mountain bike. I couldn't make out what they were saying.

Note to self: purchase instructional video entitled, "How to Read Lips."

"Be right back," said Will. His hand warned me back like a crossing guard, then he followed Kurt inside the open garage that was all organized and neat, lawn chemicals and bug sprays standing in a perfect line across white shelves, yard tools hanging evenly on wall hooks, not one speck of dirt on any of them.

At least some things seemed on the straight and narrow around here.

Kurt hit a button on the wall. The door came down like a slow-motion guillotine.

Ka-whump.

I put my left hand to my throat, then forced a swallow.

I stepped closer. The big square windows were filled with smoky glass. All I could make out was the fuzzy outline of a lightbulb hanging from the ceiling.

Should I go inside? Demand to know what's going on? Ask why I'm not invited? Read them their rights?

While I was busy planning my strategy, the door raised up again.

Kurt was leaning on the back end of the Jeep, then he fixed his baby blues on mine.

My face went hot. I pried my eyes off of him, then skimmed the room for Will. There he was, slumped in a dark corner against the workbench.

"Let's go, Sky," he said, dangling his keys in front of him like a noose.

His eyes were tiny marshmallows.

I looked over at Kurt, who was still watching me, then I shot my gaze back at Will.

"How about I drive? You can relax," I said.

"Dontcha trust me?" he asked.

If I stay back, if I let him go off by himself, who knows what will happen? And we'd be heading right home. Only a few blocks.

Plus, who wants to look like a Kentucky Fried Chicken in front of Kurt?

Not moi.

He opened the driver's door and waved me inside.

"The lock's jammed on your side," he mumbled.

I wondered about Kurt, but I avoided his face. Then I folded myself inside.

I braced myself on the steering wheel and cleared the stick shift, then landed on the fake velvet seat.

Will got in after me. He shut the door, locked it, then rolled down the window.

I felt like we were back in the womb, with Will blocking the closest emergency exit.

"Come by later," Will directed Kurt, then he jerked the gearshift in reverse.

I leaned forward, looking for a sign from Kurt, something that said "Be careful" or "Don't worry" or "I'll save you."

But his face was erased by the dusty windshield as we backed down the driveway and took off down the street.

Scene 32

I wished we had the Driver's Ed car, the one with the passenger-side brake, antilock, and the yellow sign on top warning: "Caution: Student Driver."

Only our sign would say: "Caution: Stoner Driver."

Then maybe someone would stop us, call 9-1-1, send out the rescue dogs, the big drooly ones with root-beer barrels under their chins.

"Will, take it easy, what's the hurry?" I said, avoiding any verbal whitecaps.

I could feel his energy rising like he was a guitar amp, his volume cranking up to ten.

One more notch and it's "Stairway to Heaven."

"Maybe we should get home. Mom's probably wondering," I said.

"Yeah, wondering whether she should kiss Ed Dickey's left butt cheek or his right," Will said, "I'm never going back there, not if I can help it."

He seemed completely lost, like he had no idea where he was or where he could possibly go from here.

Dead end.

How could I bail on him now? He needed some time to get a grip, to settle down.

"Let's drive around a little then, maybe we can talk about it, you can figure out what to do," I said. "But why don't you let me drive?"

"No, I'm fine," he said. "I can drive."

Then he pushed the pedal to the metal, making all four tires cry out in pain.

I scrunched my eyes closed, white-knuckling the edge of my seat.

"Hey Will, chill out a little," I said, my voice pressing the panic button.

He eased it up a bit. Maybe I hadn't lost him yet.

"Forget it Will. Let's just go home, okay?"

He answered by stepping on the gas.

"Relax," he said, just like my dentist before he reclines the chair, swings over the drill.

r-r-r-r-R-R-R-R-**R-R-R-R-R**!

Only this time, there's no laughing gas.

"Where are you going?" I said, trying to stay calm.

"Let's go for a ride."

We were heading outside of town, taking the back way toward the bridge. Before I knew it, we were on the twisty wooded road everyone in Red Creek called Thirteen Curves. The one that was always the setting for the spooky story where the boyfriend finds his date hanging from a tree, her head chopped off.

I had enough. This was out of my league.

"I don't want to go," I said, my voice firm. "Take me home."

Nonchalant. Nonthreatening. Nonmotivating.

The headlights flashed across a yellow sign yelling, "Danger: Curves Ahead," a thick black line curling like ribbon candy.

I read my fate.

"Will, turn around, go back," I begged in a voice that would've gotten down on two knees if it had legs.

He seemed to not hear me.

We entered a dark tunnel of trees.

He took the first bend to the right, throwing me to the left.

Before I could get my balance, he hit the second curve, jerking the wheel to the left, flinging me to the right, my shoulder slamming up against the door handle.

I counted the curves like nails in a coffin, and I cried out as he hammered every one.

3, 4, 5, 6, 7, ...

But all he did was step on it even more.

I am trapped. I want this to end. I'll do whatever it takes.

But all I could do was sit there and hang on.

Tears burned my face like liquid metal.

8, 9, 10, ...

My rag-doll body pitched from side to side, over and over again.

The Jeep, faster, faster, faster.

I couldn't stay here. I had to get out.

I saw myself grip the door handle and pull it, then slam my bruised shoulder against the door, once, then again, harder.

Jammed. The broken lock.

11, 12,…

No escape.

I reached over and grabbed the wheel.

"Let me go, you're messing me up," he said.

13.

The Jeep lurched, then tipped on two wheels as it swerved across the double yellow line, headlights stabbing the black trees, now, now, now.

The world bouncing around me, we crossed into the oncoming lane, blind to other cars that might be heading for a collision with us.

Will let out an animal cry, his fingers prying mine away from the wheel like fishhooks.

"Sky, get away! Let me do it!"

His body rammed back at me, then forward against the horn, sounding an alarm that no one could hear but Will and me, muffling my scream as we flew head-on into a giant tree.

Scene 33

Dead silence. A rigor mortis stillness. Our rest in peace.

I wondered if that meant we were goners.

I opened my eyes.

Dark leaves covered the windshield.

We just missed the tree.

I clicked on the map light, then surveyed the interior landscape.

I cut off my breath.

Will looked like crash-test dummy Andy, slumped over the steering wheel.

Is he dead or alive?

A short breath caught in my throat, a sense of doom washing over me like I was in an emotional car wash, those giant soapy hula skirts trapping me inside.

A groan.

I reached out to Will, then pushed him back gently.

A trickle of blood sliced an *S* down his cheek.

Stupid.

Sick.

Save me.

He opened his eyes halfway.

"You could have gotten me killed," he muttered like he was talking in his sleep.

ME? Gotten HIM killed?

Excuse me, waitress? Could you bring my brother the reality check, please?

"Sky, I'm not ready to die," he said, then his eyelids closed like the final curtain.

My face went hot as I turned away, wondering if the old Will was still living, if the real Will was already dead.

I climbed into the backseat, then jockeyed Will into the passenger's seat. Then I scaled back over into the driver's seat and took my place behind the wheel.

I took a deep breath and slipped the Jeep into reverse.

I sent out a quick prayer to the Goddess of Lost Causes, then gunned it.

"C'mon, baby," I pleaded.

Rubber grabbed dirt, rocketing us backward, straight out of the woods and back to the Land of Who Knows What's Next.

Scene 34

Will was out of it, sagging down in the seat like a sack of Idaho potatoes the whole way home. Instead of keeping my eyes on the road, I kept them on Will, glancing over every two seconds to make sure he was still breathing.

Worries swam through my head and multiplied like amazing sea monkeys.

How will I sneak him inside? If we get caught, what will Mom say? What should I say back? How do I save Will's butt, and my own butt, too? And what about Ed?

I punched off the headlights and pulled up the driveway, maneuvering around Ed's car, into the garage.

The night was thick and warm. Every breath was like sucking in air through a wet towel.

I stepped outside the garage. The kitchen light was on.

Maybe they're eating microwave popcorn. They could be smiling and laughing, playing The Game of Life. Maybe Mom's happy because she's winning. She has a little pink peg and a little blue one, too, sitting behind her own pink peg in her little plastic car. The green one.

Her own little perfect Game of Life family.

It could be they forgot all about Will and the smashed-in wall. And when they see us, maybe they'll invite us to join in their fun, just like nothing happened, like any trouble is permanently struck from the record.

"Where is he?" hissed Ed's rattlesnake voice behind me.

I swiveled to my left and saw the silhouette of Ed leaning against the garage, his hands in his pockets, all casual-like.

"Ed, you scared me. Don't scare me like that," I said, feeling my pounding heart, my twitchy smile. "Where's Mom?"

It was like he didn't hear me, like his Miracle-Ear was in the "off" position.

"What'd you do with him?" he said, stepping toward me, coming out of the shadows.

I went a step backward, he took another toward me.

"What are you talking about?"

"Your brother, where's he hiding?"

I took another step back. He stepped toward me again.

This was a life-size chess match, and Ed was winning.

"Everything is okay, you don't need to get involved," I said.

"Your mother's so upset she can't get out of bed."

I thought about calling for her, possibly screaming my about-to-explode head off, but her room was on the other side of the house, and her air conditioner would block out any sound.

No matter what, she wouldn't hear me.

"Ed, take it easy."

"Now I get it. He's killing your mother, and you're his partner in crime."

"What are you talking about?"

"You're just as much to blame."

He moved toward me, one step, two, then three. I backed into the hedges. They clawed the back of my legs.

Checkmate.

The Jeep door slammed. Ed turned back to face the sound.

Will came out from the garage.

"You heard her, Ed," said Will, staking out his territory that was right next to me. "Back off."

"Well look at that, if it isn't the life of the party himself," sneered Ed.

"Get the hell out of here," Will said.

"Oh, now you're Mister Big Shot. You better get one thing straight—I'm not going anywhere."

"That's what you think," said Will.

"You two have a lot to learn," said Ed, then he went into the house and turned off the kitchen light.

Scene 35

The next morning, Mom was sitting at the kitchen table in her pink terrycloth bathrobe, the one with the French poodles and Eiffel Tower appliqués. Curly black script spelled out, "Ooh la la." Her fuzzy slippers made her feet look like purple eyelashes. She was drinking her decaf, doing her crossword puzzle.

I stood across the table from her, my arms folded across my chest.

The Baxter family hall monitor.

"How are you this morning, sunshine?" she sang like a songbird.

Sunshine? How about total solar eclipse?

Enough is enough.

"Mom, how can you act like everything is okay? Like Will isn't a mess?"

"Of course I'm concerned about your brother, Sky. I couldn't be more worried," she said. And it sounded like she meant it. "But based on my obvious, multiple failures dealing with your father, I've decided we need help from someone else, somebody who knows what to do and is willing to take action. That's why I'm relying on Ed. He has many more successes in this area than I could ever hope for."

"But, Mom, Ed has cats! He doesn't have a freakin' clue about people!" I cried.

"He's already started to take charge, and we need to appreciate him for that," she said.

Case closed.

"What's an eight-letter word for 'disaster'?" she asked.

"Try 'E D D I C K E Y,' " I said.

Talk about a mood killer.

Mom looked up, glaring at me over her pink half-glasses.

"Sky, why do you have to be so negative? Ed could be the best thing that's ever happened to this family, for all you know."

"He's too bossy. He thinks he's in charge," I stated, using my expert voice.

"A strong hero always does the unknotting, propels the denouement," she said like she was standing at the overhead projector.

"Mother, this is not a romance novel. It's our real life." I heard myself pleading now.

"I am simply trying to get you to see the possibilities."

She was losing her patience, exasperated by my ignorance.

I glanced out the window. Ed's car was gone.

I wasn't ready to give up.

"Didn't he tell you what happened last night?"

"As a matter of fact he most certainly did. We have no secrets. He said he had to immediately lay down the law with Will. His words exactly."

"Is that what he said? You let him get away with a cliché? And a split infinitive, too?"

"Yes, and in fact, I thanked him for it."

My jaw dropped. Thanked him for it?

"Will requires structure. Someone needed to take immediate action. Sky, he's out of control, you know it and I know it. What's the alternative?"

The question was a brick wall. The smorgasbord of alternatives: jail, house arrest, headline news, rehab, six feet under.

"Ed's really controlling, he's too harsh," I said, my voice mousy, totally unconvincing.

If this were a screen test, I would never get the part.

"We just aren't used to having a man around the house. He's doing what any real man would do: taking charge. It's exactly what Will needs."

I just stared at her.

"That is, unless you have a better idea," she shot at me.

Her words were a verbal stun gun. When I came to, I sat down next to her and looked at her puzzle.

"Try 'collapse,'" I said.

"Perfect! It fits!"

Then I just sat there, watching her scribble the letters one by one into those teensy little crossword squares.

Scene 36

Cat was already there waiting for me when I got to the bridge. I can always count on her to respond promptly and swiftly to my 9-1-1 calls.

I plopped down next to her on the grass. She was sitting on her "Welcome to Sunny Florida" beach towel, one of the matching ones we picked up last summer at the dollar store.

"It's really bad, isn't it?" said Cat.

I always feel better after telling Cat anything. Maybe that's because she's the only one who ever really listens. Not to mention the fact she's the only human in my crazy world with half a brain.

"I thought our sixteenth summer was going to be the best ever, everyone said so," I said.

"Hey, look at the bright side. There's six weeks left before school starts. Still time for things to turn around."

"Yeah, maybe Kurt will fall madly in love with me. And Will, he'll become an Eagle Scout. And Ed Dickey will get transferred to East Katmandu."

Cat laughed, and I caught myself cracking a smile.

I threw back my head and closed my eyes, soaking up the sun through my eyelids that looked red-orange from the inside.

"Let's take a dip," Cat offered.

I pulled off my T-shirt, uncovering my bathing suit, then followed Cat's giant running steps and her high-speed windmill arms into the river.

Cat stopped and planted herself when the water reached the top of her shoulders. I waded over until I was right next to her.

Then she looked up to the heavens and started yelling in this revival meeting preacher voice: "Someone cleanse this innocent young person, please!"

She fluttered her eyelids like she was in some kind of spiritual trance.

Her right hand grabbed my left, then she yanked it up toward the sky.

"You are crazy!" I laughed.

"Wash away this poor girl's misery!" Cat continued.

"Cat! What are you—"

The water drowned my words as she dunked me, while she went under, too.

We opened our eyes underwater, holding each other's shoulders, Cat looking at me and me at her, both of us smiling. Her hair floated around her head like a golden crown.

Then we popped back up again.

"Let's have a party," Cat said.

"When? Where?" I asked.

"In the bomb shelter. Tonight," said Cat, like it was the most natural idea in the world. "I'll invite Will and Kurt. We can show them a good time without any of the nasty stuff."

I thought about it for a second. Maybe that's the perfect idea, having fun together without the aid of artificial enhancements, just like old times.

"Why not? Better than shriveling up for the evening, which was basically all I had planned for myself."

"I guess the cleansing worked," she said smiling.

Then she held up her hands to the sky, looking up, shifting into that preacher voice again. "My friend has found her lost soul. Thank you, healing water spirits!"

"Cut it out!" I laughed.

I dunked Cat, her face surprised, then swam my fastest back to shore before she could catch me.

VIDEO DIARY,  ENTRY SEVEN

VIDEO: *Vertical Wipe to MEDIUM SHOT of SELF. SELF is sitting on futon in bomb shelter, wearing bleached-out overalls and orange tank top with multicolored beads around edging. SELF'S hair is pulled straight up into fish barrette, creating Old Faithful eruption effect.*

AUDIO: Just a few words before Party Time, Unlimited. And no, I'm not done getting myself ready, as you can tell by observing my own personal fashion emergency. I'd like to send a big shout out to Cat for coming up with the idea of having a party in the first place. I'm not exactly sure what she has up her sweatshirt sleeve for this particular night, but I can tell by that look on her face that it's more than just her favorite flannel undergarment. And her Big Plan could very possibly start with a capital *K* and end with a capital *T*, with a capital *U R* stuck right there in between. If I am correct, let me say: bring it on! And here's what else I'm thinking: maybe we can show Will a squeaky clean good time. Maybe we can have the kind of fun we used to have, the pre-pill and booze laughs that used to feel so easy.

Enough talk. Time to do the Cinderella act, so I can start hoping for a little magic tonight. Before I turn into a pumpkin.

Insert spfx: magic wand drops into picture, waves itself, sparkles fall, image disappears.

Scene 37

I spread out the snack buffet on the generator in the corner of the room.

Dipsy Doodles (rippled) in a napkin-lined basket, M&M's (plain) in my Sponge Bob cereal bowl, Strawberry Twizzlers (bite-size) on a dessert plate, Doritos (ranch flavor) next to a tea cup loaded with French-onion dip.

"Miss, may I interest you in our newest-style coffee table?" I said to Cat in my shopping channel voice. "When you're not using it for entertaining, it doubles as a power source. Guaranteed to make your response to global crisis more comfortable…"

"…or your money back, that is, if the generator store isn't nuked first," said Cat.

She slid a CD into the boom box and clicked play.

Background music: "If loving you is wrong, I don't wanna be right...."

"I told Will, just come to the party, no funny business. Be straight and we'll have fun, just like the old days," I said to Cat.

"His first step to recovery, right? Dipsy Doodles and Twizzlers."

"You got it, we're in a no-fly zone," I said.

The bomb shelter door squeaked open.

"Honey, I'm home!" called Will's voice.

"Did you remember the milk and eggs?" Cat shouted up.

"Of course not, but I brought a friend with me for dinner. I hope it's okay."

"It's all I live for, entertaining your friends on a moment's notice, sweetheart," said Cat.

Will's footsteps clunked down the stairs, then Kurt's.

I snapped a mental Polaroid of Kurt. His emerald green muscle shirt. His adorable mussed-up hair. His incredibly cute half-smile. His jeans faded to a perfect baby blue.

Insert: emotional logjam.

Lucky me. Petrified wood.

Cut to General Hospital *sound stage.*

NURSE (with intensity): "Doctor, this patient has a severe case of true-love paralysis...yet she's only spoken two words to him in her entire sorry life!"

DOCTOR (with conviction): "Prognosis: pathetic!"

Insert sfx: dramatic organ music.

Cut to dish detergent commercial.

Back to reality.

"Time to play Twister!" Cat yelled.

She unfolded the plastic sheet and spread it across the bomb shelter floor. I looked at the giant tiddlywink circles: red, green, yellow, blue. The sight of them gave my stomach a queasy, you-went-overboard-on-the-Tootsie-Rolls feeling.

"Sky, you and Kurt go first," she said, grabbing the spinner.

Kurt and I looked at each other. My face felt like a marshmallow being toasted over a bonfire, and someone was holding me way too close to the flame. We took our places, opposite each other.

"Right foot green," she called.

We followed orders.

"Left hand yellow."

My hand went down on the circle next to his. No body contact.

"Left foot blue."

Kurt reached for the far circle, so our legs brushed up against each other.

Okay, I can handle that.

"Right hand red."

His hand reached over my foot. His shoulder pressed against my hip.

I dropped down my head, my hair covering my face where every ounce of my blood was collecting.

"Left foot red."

We swung our legs over, our bodies all contorted and rubbery now.

Kurt was Gumby. I was Pokey.

"Left hand yellow."

Kurt's hand slid between my feet, my arm went over him, his head in the crook of my arm.

My knees started to shake, then my body. I toppled over and landed on my butt.

"Sky, you lose!" said Will. "C'mon Cat. Our turn."

I got myself over to the futon and collapsed, while Kurt picked up the spinner.

"Right foot blue," he said.

Then I closed my eyes and listened to Will and Cat play around, while those red, green, yellow, blue circles swirled inside my head like giant juggling balls I was fighting not to drop.

Scene 38

"Gotta fly," said Cat, consulting the Rugrats watch she bought for a buck at Burger King. "Time is so fleeting in Twister heaven."

"I'll walk you," said Will. "Be back in a few."

An hour was more like it. A long walk with Cat would do Will good. He appeared to be at least semi-straight tonight, so maybe Cat could talk to him, drive some sense into him, maybe she would say the right thing. Maybe she could make a difference in his life, and mine, too, while she's at it.

Before I finished the thought, Will and Cat were gone, and it was just Kurt and me.

Alone at last.

Big gulp. And I'm not talking the 7-Eleven kind.

"Where's Michelle?"

Insert sfx: glass shattering.

Brilliant line of questioning, Sky.

Not!

"We broke up."

Cha-ching! Flashing lights! Happy sirens! You just hit the jackpot, lucky lady!

"Oh, sorry," I said.

"Don't be. It's all okay."

Kurt moved closer, then sat next to me on the futon, moving his body to face me.

This warm and sweet maple syrupy feeling dripped over me. I pushed back my head, then set it straight again, turning in slow motion to take in the blueness of his eyes. He looked back at me. It seemed he saw deep inside me, and me inside him, and for the first time it felt fine, natural and real, with everything just right.

Kurt rested his left hand on mine, then moved it to my elbow, pushing his fingers a little inside the sleeve of my shirt, then starting to tickle, gently, the skin underneath. His right hand slid across my other hand, down the soft underside of my arm, up around my waist.

Goose bumps followed every inch of his touch.

Then he leaned into me, I felt his soft lips press against mine. I closed my eyes and eased into him, my body a floating cloud. I felt his tenderness, taking in his breath as if it were my own.

Then I felt him pull away.

"Nice," he whispered.

"Yes, nice," I whispered back, opening my eyes.

Is this really him? Is this really me with him?

If this is a dream, do not disturb. Do not, I repeat, do not, wake me up.

"I need to hook up with someone fifteen minutes ago," he said. "How about tomorrow night? Can I come back?"

"I'll be here," I said.

Kurt threw on his jacket, then scrambled up the stairs.

After the door closed, I squeezed my knees to my chest, wrapping my arms around them, then giggled and threw back my head, letting myself believe that something good might actually happen to me this summer after all.

Scene 39

"What?!" cried Cat, sitting next to me, her arms hugging the man-of-steel girders of the bridge that reminded me of a giant black cat, arching its back high above the water.

"It's true! Kurt kissed me!" I said. "And he's coming back to be with me tonight," I said slowly, accentuating every word to achieve the appropriate dramatic effect.

Cat didn't say a word.

"Maybe it'll be the special night when I finally lose the scarlet *V*."

I thought, she must be so excited, she doesn't know what to say.

Too bad there isn't a manual: *101 Clever Quips When Your Best Friend's in Love.*

Then I saw Cat's back walking away from me.

"Hey, where you going?" I said, grabbing both soggy towels. "Wait up," I called out, following after her as she bolted off the bridge.

I caught up with her on the path in the woods. The pine trees bent over us like those enormous feather fans they use in those harem movies.

"Cat, what's wrong?"

"I guess I didn't know everything would be moving this fast," she said, hurt buried deep inside her words. "Hey, don't worry about it. You can spend all your free time with Kurt, and I'll still have me, myself, and I to hang out with."

She kept walking. I stayed with her, grabbed her shoulder, pulled it, her, toward me.

"Cat, I don't get it. You're the one who set it up. You made it happen. If it wasn't for you…" I started.

"Hey, don't remind me. I'm a real expert at setting myself up to be alone. How genius of me."

Her red eyes looked off to the side, far away, too distant from me.

What did I do? The thought of hurting Cat fell on me like a giant asteroid.

Squish.

"Cat…"

She bit her lip, kept looking down, her words stuck someplace deep inside.

I wondered why she looked like someone had just carried out a sneak attack on her, and how it so happened that someone was me.

Raise the white flag. Let's call a truce.

"Why does everything have to change?" she forced out.

I wanted to fill up the space put there by me, but I didn't know how.

"Things won't change, Cat. I promise," I said, wishing I could get her to believe me, wondering how I could do it.

"It's Dad and Susan. I heard them talking last night. About splitting up."

Oh boy.

"You think I'd be jumping for joy," she said, knowing she was doing anything but.

I realized Cat wasn't Susan's number one fan. But Susan had been around for a while. A lot longer than her very own mother had. Maybe Cat was more tied to Susan than I had thought, or Cat had thought, too.

"This is stupid, all of it," she said. "I gotta go."

I wanted to say the right thing, to let her know that nothing would interfere with our friendship. Not now. Not ever. That I'd help her deal with her father and Susan. That she could count on me. Now and forever.

But before I could get it out, she took off, running, while I stood there trying to wrap my brain around the last few minutes that had just stolen away my best friend.

VIDEO DIARY,  ENTRY EIGHT

VIDEO: *Fade up to MEDIUM SHOT of SELF, FLAT OUT on BED, BELLY-FLOPPER STYLE, HANDS PROPPING UP HEAD.*

AUDIO: Okay. Progress report. How do I add things up? Dust off the mental calculator. Me plus Kurt plus Cat equals trouble. Me plus Kurt, minus Cat equals sad. Me plus Cat, minus Kurt equals disappointment. I can't get it to add up. Maybe that's my problem. I always stunk at math. Here I am, the afternoon before Kurt could be knock, knock, knockin' on heaven's door, the most defining moment of my sixteen years on the planet, and all I can think of is what Cat might think, how it might change everything between us. However, she did set us up. Kind of. And on the other side of the quadratic equation is how I might never get the chance with Kurt now. Or ever. Just me, Kurt, the futon. Utopia.

Why can't things be simple for once? Forget math, try the artistic approach. How do I frame this scene? Give me a visual. Remember the rule of threes. Recall the perfect harmony of the golden triangle. Its roots in nature. The perfect relationship has three sides: Cat, Kurt, and me. Yes, I can have it all.

I just realized why I love art.

Later.

VIDEO: *Horizontal wipe to black screen.*

Scene 40

Flecks of silver disco ball light danced across me as I lay back on the futon. The dark room was a shadow box, like the Romeo and Juliet one I made in fifth grade that just popped into my head.

The boom box was crying out the Rolling Stones.

"You can't always get what you want."

Kurt, where is Kurt?

Thoughts of Cat weighed down on me like the lead apron at the dentist's office.

Kurt, where is Kurt?

I called her three times today. No answer. Nobody home.

Kurt, where is Kurt?

Tomorrow I am taking myself there, I will show up at her door, it will be me, right there, in the flesh. *Ding-dong.* Here I am. You can't get rid of me so quickly.

I'll say, Cat, you need to let me go.

I'll say, Cat, you need to let me hang on.

I heard the door pull open.

"You down there?" came Kurt's voice, popping the Cat thought-bubble like a straight pin.

I jolted myself to the upright position like an airplane tray table, smoothed down my hair, pulled down my shirt.

"Yes," I whispered like I was saying something no one should hear.

When he came into view, my stomach capsized.

Girl overboard.

"Hey," I said, singing it like I was auditioning for the school chorus.

Cool your jets. Get a grip. Plant size eights firmly on the ground.

My heart: *pa-bump, pa-bump, pa-bump.*

"Hey," he said back.

He floated over, sat down close next to me, taking my hand from my lap, wrapping it inside his warm hands that felt so soft on the underside.

The nervousness ran right out of me.

Am I ready for this? Is it time to vacate the pristine palace of innocent, nubile virgins?

Yes.

Yes.

Yes.

He leaned back, resting his head against the silky tangerine pillow with beads dangling like tiny icicles around the edges. He smiled up at me.

A freeze-frame moment if I ever saw one.

Then we pulled toward each other, my body drawn to his, a drop of water falling to the ground, an irresistible force of nature.

Interpersonal gravity.

"Sir Isaac Newton would be proud," I said.

"Huh?" he said, popping back his head.

"Nothing. Never mind." I pulled him back into me.

I breathed in his scent—Ivory soap?—while he gave me little kisses all over my face, my neck, my ear, his mouth tickling my skin like tiny feathers.

That's when I felt his Earth start to move in the Land Down Under.

I took his face in my hands and turned it toward me, our noses bumped over each other, our lips found each other.

I felt my breathing, and Kurt's, too, fast and shallow.

My head felt light, crackling with thousands of electric sparks.

There was a desire to move quickly, a desire to go slow, a desire to suspend ourselves in time, to be in this place forever.

Our hands read each other's bodies.

And it all felt so nice.

Real nice.

We were exploring my uncharted territory.

"Go West, young man," I whispered, startled to hear myself say it aloud.

"What'd you say?" Kurt whispered back.

I giggled. "Nothing, I'm just happy, that's all," I said.

Kurt smiled.

I felt my face hot, red, full of fire. Kurt's sweet breath washed over me like summer air.

I surrender.

We shifted to our sides, lying face-to-face, kissing, touching, kissing some more, please don't stop, our bodies in a deep, slow motion, a sleepy sensual mating dance, we moved to each other's rhythms.

One by one, our clothes parachuted to the ground, mounds of fabric piling up like the Himalayas.

Time to mount the high peak.

Let the ascent begin.

I pulled the afghan over us, and there we were inside, skin-to-skin, mouth-on-mouth, an avalanche of desire more powerful than either of us, shifting our positions, overtaking us both.

Scene 41

So how did it go, my first trip to the Hotel of Ecstasy? The Erotic Econolodge of No Return?

Turns out the Mediocre Motel was more like it.

Was that it? The whole shebang?

The boom box sneered: "I can't get no, satisfaction."

Thanks for rubbing it in, Mick.

Was that my so-called defining moment? My sexual awakening?

Welcome to Snoozeville was more like it.

I looked over at Kurt, presently a citizen of Snoozeville himself.

How could he sleep at a moment like this?

And how could something this important, this monumental, this personally historic, be over practically before it started?

Our trip to paradise, and we barely made it out of the driveway.

And on top of that, it didn't tickle.

You try forcing a carrot inside a Cheerio.

Believe me, you wouldn't want to be the Cheerio.

Even if you're talking a baby carrot.

For a second, I thought about the new me. The one who was forever altered, the one who could never return to the garden of unplucked flower buds.

Face the truth.

I am already cut, dried, and smushed inside the pages of the Encyclopedia Britannica. I belong stuck in volume *T*, right there alongside Titanic. Tsunami. Tuberculosis.

Accept it.

Maybe I set my sights too high.

But people in the movies really get into it. They're screaming and moaning and throwing themselves all over each other like there's no tomorrow.

Maybe that's why they call it acting.

"You okay?" Kurt stretching, then turning his head to face me.

His eyes were wide, they were saying "I wanted to please you," they were searching for a thumbs-up, some hopeful sign of approval. Anything to acknowledge his entry into the wonderful world of young manhood.

That's when my brain did a 180. That's when I realized we were traveling in this uncertain universe together.

I wriggled my shoulder under his head, put my arm around his neck, his crazy bed-head hair tickling my chin.

We need to give it time. Expertise doesn't happen overnight. Even Michelle Kwan had to start somewhere, probably skating on frozen mud puddles in her backyard.

Rome wasn't built in a day.

Practice makes perfect.

"I have to go," he said.

Insert sfx: ear-shattering record scratch.

But what about the holding part? The part when we tell each other our deepest, darkest secrets? The part when you kiss my ear and whisper that you can't wait until the next time, and I'm all that you can think about, even in your dreams?

I wanted to say: You're going to miss all of that. It won't be the same without you.

But nothing came out.

I watched him hopping into his pants, shoving his bare feet into his shoes.

"Call you sometime?" he said.

Sometime? What time?

"Yeah, sure," I said, with a weak smile.

Yeah, sure, I thought, with a broken heart.

Then I turned my face to the wall, closing my wet eyes, listening to his muddy shoes slap up the stairs in a rhythm that made it sound like he was running.

Scene 42

I lay there for I-don't-know-how-long, the disco light twirling and whirling, me tumbling, all dizzy and sick, trapped inside a spin cycle of confusion.

Was I expecting too much?

Was the disappointment all my fault? Maybe I should have studied the *Cosmo* sexual Q & A a little more seriously.

The Big O.

The Big Zero is more like it.

What about Kurt? How did he like it? Or not? Did he regret it all? Wish he hadn't bothered?

And where do we go from here? Anywhere? Nowhere? Some-place in between?

It wasn't regret that I felt. I just had to think about it all, to figure out what it meant, to make sense of it all.

Some time to myself was what I needed.

"Sky, is that you down there?"

No, not my mother. Not here. Not now.

"I hear the music. She's down there, for sure."

No, not Will, too. Not here. Not now.

"Hang on a second," I shouted, my voice impatient, my body slipping back into my wrinkled up clothes.

Then I pushed myself up, feeling wetness on my hand, seeing red streaks like claw marks across the futon, each one cut with my own blood.

A chill crawled through my body.

That's all I need—to let Mom and Will see the evidence.

I draped the flesh-colored afghan over the blood like a giant Band-Aid.

Then there they were, Will and my mother, staring down at me from the stairs like I was the subject of some kind of strange psychological experiment, a straitjacketed nutcase

behind a two-way mirror. A sensory-deprived rat trapped inside a maze.

"We've been looking everywhere for you," she said, marching
over to me, making me feel three inches tall looking up at her.

Motherly advice is exactly what I don't need right now. But I
feel it coming on, as sure and unwelcome as the common cold.

"Will finally told me you might be here, but I said, 'No, not Sky,'
she wouldn't do that, she knows this isn't a place to fool around
in. She understands this is serious business down here."

I shot my eyes to Will, but he avoided my look.

My look that said, thanks a lot, stoolie. Tattletale. Rat fink.
Squealer.

After all I've done for him. After all my cover girl cover-ups. No
wonder he couldn't look me in the eye.

"What went on down here?" my mother said, her springs
wound tight. "Just look at you, look at this mess."

If you only knew.

"Nothing happened, just nothing," I said.

But that didn't stop her. Not one little bit. "We saw Kurt leaving.
He didn't do anything he shouldn't have, now, did he?"

I just stared at her. She bulldozed on.

"Tell us what happened, Sky, you can trust us. We're a family."

That's when it hit me.

My mother's accusations, her denials, her pattern of ignorant bliss that bordered on deceit, stung me like frayed live wires, burning my skin, shocking me to my bones.

Enough.

I jerked myself up, leaped off the futon, stood at attention.

"A family?" I said, my mocking voice, my words razor-sharp. "You call this a family?"

I was laughing now, borderline crying, my Frankenstein body rigid, tense. Was I popping my cork, losing my mind?

Start the drumroll. Bring on the brutal honesty. Let the rage begin.

"Trust you? How do you expect me to trust you?" I sneered. "You can't even run your own lives, you think I'd let you get any-where near mine?"

"Sky, don't say things you don't mean, things you can't take back," my mother begged.

"She's right, Sky," Will chimed in.

I chuckled.

His intent was clear as a church bell. He was afraid of what he might hear, terrified that I might speak the truth. The truth about him, right then and there.

Nothing could stop me now. The elevator cables were cut. We were plummeting to the basement.

Too late to exit. All aboard. No one gets off until the end of the line.

I aimed the first shot at my mother: "Take a look at yourself, your boyfriend hates your own kids, but you're so wrapped up in his little pathetic world, you're clueless. You couldn't care less."

Then a shot at Will: "And you, you can't admit you have a problem. You're heading straight for burnout hell. Hey, maybe you've already arrived, and you don't even know it."

I put my mother in my crosshairs one last time: "You built this place to save us from the outside world, to protect us from all of its dangers, but the bombs are exploding in this crazy family. And the funny thing is, you won't see it, you won't hear it, you won't assess the damage. You're too afraid to look."

We were suddenly perfect strangers.

We gave each other the once-over, then we went quiet, like we were at a funeral where nobody knows what to say, where speaking is taboo.

"Cat's father's been calling, something's happened, they can't find her, she's missing," Will said. "That's why I told Mom. That's why we were looking for you."

My body went stiff.

Cat.

Missing.

Hurt.

Dying.

Dead.

Please, not Cat.

"That's all we know," came my mother's P.S.

Then I heard myself say, "Cat. I need to find Cat."

I ran up the stairs and rushed out the door, with Will trailing close behind me.

Scene 43

We hopped into the Jeep, me in the driver's seat, Will sliding in over me, him riding shotgun. After the last driving fiasco, I wasn't letting Will drive anytime soon.

"The bridge, she has to be at the bridge," I said out loud, sounding to myself like I was in a cave, my voice echoing, crashing against the walls.

"Was it Kurt?" Will said, his words sizzling.

"What are you talking about?" I said, slamming on the verbal breaks.

"Kurt, I know it was him, he was down there with you, messing with you," he said.

I pulled the Jeep over, looped my arm over the steering wheel, spun toward him.

"This isn't about you," I said. "It's about me, apart from you, I can make my own choices. Just like you did, like you do."

My words were raw and tough. Meat on a stick.

Freeze frame: close-up of Will and me, facing each other.

Insert voice-over and bulleted text (animated, left to right transition):

- CONJOINED TWINS SEPARATED AT AGE SIXTEEN
- OPERATION'S SUCCESS STILL IN QUESTION
- TWO LIVES HANG IN BALANCE

When we got to the park, he pulled a baggie out of his shirt pocket. It crackled like a brushfire as he opened it up. He took out some pills, Goddess knows what, popped them into his mouth like Sweet Tarts, threw back his head.

Down the hatch.

I felt like I was finally cracking up. At this point maybe it's the only way to go. I heard myself making one of those funhouse kind of laughs.

"It just takes off the edge, is that so bad?" His words came at me, each one a poison dart.

"What are you doing to yourself? What's it going to take for you to stop?" I cried.

"Like you said, we can make our own choices."

"Think about how I feel, what you're doing to me," I said.

"You worry too much, you always have."

I needed to make us or break us.

I looked straight at Will, his eyes starting to glaze over. It was do or die.

"You're turning out just like Dad," I said.

There, I said it. It was out there. Let him deal with it now.

"Now I get it. I'm the evil twin? And you're the perfect daughter, the wonderful sister? The better half?"

"I never said that."

Why couldn't I get through to him?

"Admit it. You're done with me, just the way you want me done with you," he shot back.

Was there some truth in his accusations? Did part of me wish I could forget about him, wish he never existed, leave him behind?

Maybe I'm not the great sister I think I am.

I watched him turn his back on me, kick the jammed door open, slam it shut.

End of story.

"Will." My brother's name was trapped inside the Jeep, caught in a place where no one could hear it but me.

I looked in the sideview mirror, Will's image framed in black plastic, his reflection, smaller, smaller, smaller, walking out of the frame.

Then he disappeared.

Poof.

My throat swelled up, aching from the words that hadn't come out, words that would have made everything better, the ones that were just the right ones to say.

Should I roll down the window, stick out my head, call his name? Pull a U-turn? Say I'm sorry, I didn't mean it? Why don't you jump back in?

But I felt myself just sitting there instead, suspended animation.

Too late for more chances. They were all used up.

Game over. The final whistle. Everybody, grab your stuff and go home.

I yanked my purple bandana from the rearview mirror, then wiped a circle from the steam on the inside of the windshield.

I could see ahead of me. All clear. Ready for takeoff.

Next thing I knew, I saw myself driving down the road, every second moving me that much farther from Will, hopefully bringing me that much closer to Cat.

Scene 44

A hyper wind started kicking up its high heels, leaves losing their grip, coming loose from trees, spinning out of control, clouds rushing away overhead, real quick, like they just saw a ghost.

Everything all around me, my world as I knew it, was unraveling, everything I knew was coming undone.

I felt my stitches stretching, snapping, one by one.

And there was nothing I could do to stop it.

Except for finding Cat.

She can make things better, she can help me pull it together, for once and for all.

Cat.

What if she's decided she's better off on her own, or maybe with a different best friend?

Where will I be then?

Alone.

Unhinged.

Me without a lifeline, floating out in space. No oxygen.

No best friend.

All this because of me.

More precisely, because of me plus Kurt.

If I hadn't been so hung up on him, if I'd paid more attention to Cat, I'd know where she is right now. We'd be together some-how, somewhere else.

Anyplace but here.

I promise to forget him, to leave him all behind.

Just let me find Cat.

I maneuvered the Jeep down a narrow path of trees that were bending, creaking from quick blasts of dynamite wind.

No turning back.

I drove deeper into thick darkness, a giant mouth of hungry forest sucking me in, swallowing me up.

I inched the car close to a ragged tree stump, parked it, spikes of bark pointing up to the sky like giant fingers with bad arthritis.

Park.

Ignition off.

Self-talk: plan your strategy. Write your dialogue.

Only the right words will do. If I blow it now, if I say the wrong thing, all will be lost.

I rehearsed the phrases: Don't worry. I found you. I'm here. I'll save you.

P.S.: I need you to save me, too.

Please, let Cat be somewhere close by, all safe and sound.

Let me find her.

Let us be good together again.

Please.

Please.

Please.

Scene 45

A black thundercloud pulled across the late afternoon sky like a room-darkening shade.

I pushed all my weight against the car door, fighting the wicked wind, then I squeezed out, the hurricane air slamming the door behind me. Hair whipped across my face, against my eyes, making them sting and burn.

I turned into the wind, faced it head-on.

Everything looked dull, distorted. Like wearing a pair of too-thick glasses that were all fogged up.

I crossed the far side of the bridge, then doubled back down the path. Lightning came faster, thunder louder.

Still no rain.

At least not yet.

Shelter. Gimme shelter.

I looked ahead as I pulled myself up, stepping on exposed tree roots, long slippery strides taking me to a dry space underneath the bridge.

Nirvana.

I could wait out the storm here. Relax. Take it easy. You'll be okay.

Then came voices from above, dropping down on me like scud missiles.

The creek water was running loud, fast, whooshing and swirling its way downstream, so I couldn't make out the words. But I felt the death grip of their sound, pulling my insides like an undertow. I could tell these were angry words, these were fighting voices.

Kurt.

And Will.

He must've cut through the woods to beat me here.

I quit breathing.

Stop tape.

The script wasn't supposed to be written this way.

Will isn't in this scene. He was written out in the one before.

This scene is where I find Cat.

The one where we agree to be best friends forever.

Kiss, kiss. Hug, hug. All good again.

The one where she gets me back on track and tells me exactly what to do with Will.

It isn't supposed to be this way.

I gripped the steel girder, let it support me, held on for dear life.

Face it.

I am here.

Here I am.

Like it.

Or not.

Scene 46

Enter storm, stage left.

Fast motion. Warp speed.

Rain shooting down like a shower of bullets. Hard and fast. No escaping their spray.

I edged up the slope under the bridge, trying to move in closer so I could hear what they were saying.

But the muddy ground was sliding me away. I couldn't get a grip.

I lost my footing, slipping down the hill, crashing to the sandy ground. I felt pain, a sharp stone piercing my knee.

I rolled to the side, my legs slathered with mud, tattooed with patches of tiny stones, specks of dead grass, a ripple of blood streaming off to the side.

The thunder came loud, fast, an orchestra of cymbals and drums, confused, out of synch, a psychotic battle of the bands.

Then I looked up, the lightning a strobe light, figures of Will and Kurt moving all herky-jerky on top of the bridge. Right under the diamond-shaped yellow sign:

DANGER: FALLING AREA
ENTER AT YOUR OWN RISK

"I told you to keep away from her, that she's off-limits," said Will's growling voice.

"Take it easy, it's not what you think," Kurt said, backing off, a whimpering dog.

I clawed my way up higher, red mud jamming under my fingernails, the rain hammering hard, pounding wet tacks into my skin.

Will grabbed Kurt's shoulders. Their outlines teeter-tottering on the edge of the bridge. The sky spun around them, making me dizzy, weak.

One false move, it's finished. Last call. The death rattle.

Amen.

"Bullshit," said Will's sandpaper voice.

"I'm telling you, it wasn't a big deal," he said. "It's over with, man. It never was."

Not a big deal?

Over with?

Never was?

I just got dumped, and I didn't even know it.

"You're sick, she's your sister, not your daughter," fired Kurt, latching onto Will's arms, pushing back hard.

Will went at Kurt like a wild animal. They were locked up in each other, Will's arm like a noose around Kurt's neck, Kurt's leg an iron vise around Will's.

My heart went on the warpath watching them, my peripheral vision picking up the jutting rocks below, the rushing water that seemed to be calling their names.

By then I was at the side of the bridge, but they were in another time zone, a distant place, they were on the planet out-of-control, I wasn't even a tiny blip on their radar screen.

What could I do?

Was it flight or fight? Do or die?

Then I felt a hand on my shoulder.

I turned my head.

Cat.

Scene 47

Cat grabbed my arm and pulled me over to Kurt and Will.

It was like entering the perfect storm. A critical convergence of anger. Drugs. Confusion. Fear.

The wind blasted hard, loud, unmerciful. Leaves, dead and alive, swirled around us. It was like we were trapped inside a giant food processor.

Chop. Puree. Liquefy.

Will was sitting on Kurt's chest, leaning forward, pinning Kurt's arms above his head.

Kurt struggled, squirmed, but then he ran out of steam, lay down defeated.

Uncle.

"Will, stop!" I yelled.

Will looked over at me, confused, distracted, like he just woke up from a ten-year coma. In that split second, Kurt flopped around like a fish on a hook, thrashing Will to the side, then lurched toward him from behind, tackling his legs, climbing on Will's backside, pressing his face onto the steel grid walkway.

Will let out a huge groan, then pushed himself up, went in for the kill, with Kurt as his prey.

I felt sick to my stomach, groggy. Was this just a bad dream? Please let me wake up. Let this be anything but real.

We all stood too close to the edge, too exposed to the drop-off.

"Sky, help," said Cat, snapping me back.

Then we double-teamed Will, trying to yank him off Kurt, her on one side, me on the other.

"Get off him," Cat cried, her voice strained from pulling.

Together we managed to pry Will's arms away and held him back while Kurt wriggled loose, broke away, scuttled off sideways, a human hermit crab.

Free of Will, Kurt lay on the walkway.

Out of it.

Beaten.

Crushed.

Down.

And out.

A life-size bobblehead.

His mouth was bleeding, his left eye was swelling shut.

I felt sorry for him, protective even, despite his words, in spite of myself.

Even though he was a user, a player, he didn't deserve this. Not from me, not from me through Will.

Then Will walked over, towered over us all. Ready for round two.

"Go home, Will," I said, crouched down next to Kurt, my words railroad spikes of anger. "Enough. Look what you've done."

Especially to yourself.

Will.

Worn out.

Disassembled.

Too many missing parts.

Beyond repair.

Return to the manufacturer. Banished to the land of misfit boys.

He turned, grabbed his red baseball cap in his fist, and started walking away.

The rain started to ease up. So did the wind. A calm after the storm.

"Try to stand up, we'll help you, we need to get help," Cat said to Kurt, her voice gentle, kind. She could make things better, even when everything seemed hopeless, lost, terrifying.

We needed to get Kurt away from the edge of the bridge, to move him to safer ground.

The rain let up a little. He and Cat looked like shadows in the misty fog.

Kurt looped his right arm around my neck, his left around Cat's.

We started pulling him up when his left arm slipped off Cat. She went to grab him, but lost her balance, slipped back to the side.

I reached out, grasping wet air.

I let out a scream.

Then Cat disappeared.

Scene 48

I bolted up and shot to the side of the bridge.

It took all that I was, everything I had, to look over the edge.

I clenched my hands around cold steel, braced myself, pulled my body forward.

"Cat!" I screamed.

She was in the middle of the river, holding onto a rock.

She waved her free arm.

Alive.

"My leg," she yelled up. "I can't move it."

I called out to Will.

"Cat, she went over." I cried.

Will did a 180 and ran for the path.

I looked down at Kurt.

How can I leave him?

He sat up, leaned on his elbows, then pushed off on his left hand so he could get up.

"Don't worry, I can make it," he said, jerking his head toward his car parked next to the bridge.

I touched his shoulder, then ran off to rescue Cat.

Scene 49

I slipped down the slimy path with heart-pumping strides, falling once, twice, splitting my elbow open the second time. But I didn't care.

Cat. I have to help Cat.

Now's my chance to show her I'm here for her, to prove that she can count on me.

Nothing can stop me from saving her.

Nothing.

Nothing except Will.

When I got to the grassy riverbank, the very spot where Cat and I had spent a zillion hours together, I saw Will carrying her out of the water, holding her in his arms like he was carrying her over a threshold.

Tears jabbed my eyes.

It was supposed to be me. I wanted me to be the one to save her.

Why does Will always have to get in the way? How much more could he interfere with my plans? How much more could he contribute to my whole entire falling-apart life?

I tried to get Cat's attention, to make eye contact, but her face was turned, buried in Will's chest.

I took off my rain jacket, flannel part up, laid it on the ground. Will let down Cat easy, held his hand underneath her head, placed it gently on my jacket. He wriggled off his sweatshirt, draped it over Cat, tucked in the sides around her.

Hey, shouldn't it be me doing all that?

Cat's eyes were open, but she was turned away from me, her small hand holding on to her bad leg. Little moans came from her curled-up body. She was pretty banged up, but she was awake, she was alive.

I wanted to kneel down next to her and say just the right things to make her feel better while Will ran off to get help.

"Go get the Jeep," he said, no nonsense.

Huh?

Who died and made him the Big Kahuna?

And how did he shake off his drug-induced stupor so quickly?

"Drive it up to the path. Hurry. She needs a doctor."

I looked at Will, then Cat.

Freeze tag.

And I'm "It."

I ran off to follow orders.

VIDEO DIARY, 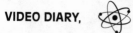  ENTRY NINE

VIDEO: *TOTALLY BLACK SCREEN. VOICE of SELF EMERGES from DARK.*

AUDIO: I thought it was me who had everything under control. Not Will. Why did he have to get it together just in time to stop me from saving Cat? The only real potential Will has in his life lately is to screw up mine. And that's just about the only potential he has no problem reaching. Good going, Will. You finally did it. You took away the person who means the most to me. What more can you do? What more?

VIDEO: *CUTS TO DISTORTION.*

Scene 50

I twisted and turned in bed that night, me, trapped in that limbo torture land between asleep and awake, between sanity and insanity. I was haunted by too many strange thoughts, every last one of them an uninvited guest.

Take off.

Leave me alone.

Not nice knowing you.

Each worry was a boomerang inside my head, crashing against my skull, dulling my senses.

I wish I had an escape hatch, a safety valve, anything to release the pressure, to set me free.

Take inventory.

Cat is okay. Check.

Kurt is okay. Check.

Will is okay. Check.

For now, anyway.

But, face it, this is only a moment in history.

A speck of lint on the overcoat of time.

Anything can happen from here on in.

The ending still needs to be written. Not to mention the denouement, the falling action.

Meanwhile, we're accidents waiting to happen, every last one of us a potential disaster. It's a proven fact.

Footnote: my sixteenth summer. Or if that's not good enough, my entire life.

I turned on my side, looked up, out the window, the sickly moon was swollen and pockmarked. Anemic, too.

Go away. Quit watching me.

Suddenly I thought about my father, wondering how things might be different if he were here. Maybe he could make things better, maybe he could take control. Maybe this was a man's job.

Then I thought, I must be dreaming.

Reality: Dad is never coming back.

Reality: I am certainly doing a lousy job of everything.

Reality: and so is everyone else in the entire Baxter family.

Reality: we're all in deep doo-doo.

I pulled up the blinds, looking out into dark nothing. And I lay there for eternity until the sun started to show up, revealing faint outlines and shadows from the Baxter family homestead, which I couldn't possibly escape, where I was forever stuck inside.

Scene 51

When I woke up the next morning after approximately two seconds of shut-eye, I thought I'd start off the day right, with some comfort food, as in a big bowl of instant oatmeal of the apple-cinnamon variety.

At least breakfast would go right today.

Wrong.

Sitting at the kitchen table, totally obstructing the cupboard containing my box of oatmeal, was none other than Ed Dickey, wearing fake silk pj's with cartoon kittens plastered all over them.

Talk about triggering an immediate loss of appetite.

I could have stayed in bed if I wanted to have a nightmare. It sure would be better than waking up to this.

"Good morning," he said. "Your mother asked me to sleep over on the sofa bed last night. She said she needed me here, under the circumstances."

I felt like saying: "You're the last person we need around here. Get lost, Ed Dickey."

But I made a grunting noise instead. I didn't have the energy to put up a fight. I only wanted my oatmeal. Just let me get my stupid oatmeal and I'll be on my way.

"Is that a proper way to respond to an adult? You could really benefit from a lesson in manners, young lady, and that brother of yours, too," he said.

Barf.

"Whatever you say, Ed," I said, sarcasm dripping from every word. "Can you move so I can get to my breakfast?"

"Obedience school wouldn't be out of the question if such a thing existed for teenagers. You need to learn to do and say what's appropriate. I hope I didn't come along too late."

Before I could appropriately stand up for myself by appropriately mouthing off to Ed Dickey, Mom entered the kitchen.

"Hello, you two," she said, plugging in the hot pot. "You're having a good conversation, I hope?"

"I'd say so, dear," Ed Dickey said, looking up at my mother, then over at me. "We were just discussing the value of a good education."

That's when I lost it. Big time.

"Ed, why don't you leave us alone? We can handle our own problems. We don't need you or your idiotic cat pajamas either."

Ed Dickey looked at me like he was choking on a hairball.

"Sky! Ed is only trying to help. You need to apologize immediately," she said.

Mom put her hand on Ed Dickey's shoulder.

Great. Now I've shown Mom that she doesn't only have Will to worry about because—Attention, everyone!—I'm out of control, too.

Two unruly teenagers for the price of one.

All the more reason for Mom to align herself with Ed Dickey.

"Skyler Baxter, you need to face it," Mom said. "We have a code-red emergency in this house. Which means we need all the reinforcements we can get. And thankfully, that includes Ed. Can we count on you, too, Sky?"

What's all this "we" stuff?

I looked at that sniveling Ed, next to my haven't-got-a-clue Mom.

Game over.

Since she is dead set on going about this in her own way, I'm dead set on going about it in mine.

"Well maybe you'd better call in the National Guard or the X-Men or Stone Cold Steve Austin because I'm out of here," I said.

I left Mom standing there, holding the hot pot with her mouth dropped open, and Ed choking on a fresh hairball, as I darted out the door.

Scene 52

I walked straight to Cat's house. I needed time to think, space to breathe.

Today's emotional agenda:

Cat and me.

Regroup. Reassess.

Would I have really put our friendship on hold?

Would I have even let it go if things with Kurt had worked out in that picture-perfect way?

Obviously, Cat thinks so. And she knows me better than I know myself.

I could have proved her wrong. I could have shown her the kind of friend I really am.

But we'll never really know since the male protagonist is history.

Wake up and smell the café latte.

I'm in this mess all because of a boy.

A dumb-ass boy who made his entrance and exit all in one day.

Hi.

Bye.

How did I really feel about Kurt? Was I in love? Really, truly?

Or was I proving I was a girl who could follow through, a girl who isn't afraid to go all the way?

Smack! Out of the ballpark.

A girl who'll step up to the plate and hit a home run?

Steeeeeeeeeeee-rike!

You're out.

Enough of the sports metaphors, already. I was at Cat's house.

No cars in the driveway. Translation: coast is clear. Come on in. Make yourself at home.

I slipped down the narrow hallway, stood outside her bedroom door.

Please, let her be here inside, all tucked away, safe and sound. Let us be good together again.

Please.

I tapped twice. "Cat?"

Insert: long pause.

I felt all flat inside, a tire without air. Where was she?

Then from inside her room, her fed-up Nurse Ratchett voice: "I'm sorry, Ms. Cat O'Connor has a long line of visitors this morning. She's our most popular patient. You'll have to take a number."

I pushed open the door.

There she was, sitting up in bed, the left side of her face a smushed purple plum, her eye a black walnut.

I sat down on the edge of her bed, slowly, gracefully, a jerky dragonfly landing on water, trying as hard as I could to prevent the ripple effect.

Cat's leg was all wrapped up in a hot pink cast, propped up on her Mighty Morphin Power Rangers pillow she'd had since we were in kindergarten. Cat seemed to keep things forever. She would never throw anything away. She always saw the good in everything. No matter how old or used up.

And that went for me, too.

I felt a gentle tug inside me.

It was time to spill the emotional beans.

"You doing okay?" was all I said.

"I figure a broken bone is the perfect way to end the summer," she said.

"And the black eye is bonus material," I said back.

"Yeah, it kind of ranks right up there with heat stroke and poison ivy."

"And maybe throw in a little jungle fever, too," I said. "The real itchy kind."

"Sounds like a good time." Cat's smile made the room feel full of light.

I thought about her ankle, how it looked when Will carried her out of the water, how it was all turned around like a used-up twistie tie.

Then I remembered the pain that was written in bold letters all over her face.

"That was a tough fall," I said, my voice turning shadowy, gloomy.

"I thought I'd start practicing for my new career," Cat said.

"And what might that be?" I asked, setting her up for the punch line.

ME: Cat's straight woman.

"Intergalactic cliff diving," she said, in all seriousness.

And we both cracked up.

Then I went quiet. I was imagining what could have happened at the bridge, how I could have lost her forever.

Snap. Just like that.

I was seeing the negative space that could have been Cat, torturing myself with thoughts of life without her.

My heart felt heavy and dark, thinking how everything could have changed, how her possible destruction came down to a matter of a few inches either way.

I thought about how there could have been no second chance.

I didn't want to think anymore.

Stop.

Rewind.

Go back to where things were, where they used to be.

Erase the recent past.

Record over it with something better, new.

But first, review the tape. Note the bad shots, the shaky edits. Eliminate inconsistencies.

Work on continuity, improve the juxtaposition.

Character development needs attention.

Listen.

Watch.

Play.

Scene 53

"So why'd you take off? How come you ran away?" I blurted out.

Translation: "What did I do wrong? Why is this all my fault?"

"Everything got to me. I just needed a break, and it looks like I got one," Cat said, pointing down at her cast.

I didn't laugh.

"Hey, that was supposed to be a joke," she whined.

I turned away, tossed my attention out the window.

"What's the matter, Sky?" she said. "Talk to me."

"Cat..."

Basically.

But the words stuck in my throat like a spoonful of Marshmallow Fluff.

Choke.

Cat took over for me.

"I shouldn't have been so weird about you, about you and Kurt. All the stuff between my father and Susan, it made me a little crazy, that's all," she said.

Cat was looking up at her vintage Bob Dylan poster. The one where his hair looks like multicolored worms.

The times, they are a changin'.

"For the record, it looks like they're okay. Susan and my father. At least for the time being," said Cat. "They're going to get some counseling, probably read some Dr. Phil, knowing Susan."

"Really? That's good news, right?"

"I guess Susan's not that bad when you add everything up," she said.

She glanced over at her dresser, everything on top lined up in a perfect row, labels facing forward. Roll-on deodorant. Baby powder. After-bath spray: Summer Breeze. Spray-on hair color: green. Glittery nail polish: purple. Every flavor of ChapStick ever known to womankind.

Some stability in Cat's unsteady world.

I wanted to tell her how scared I was when I couldn't find her.

But she said it first.

"At the bridge, I saw you there, thinking you lost me, when all the time I thought I lost you, too," she told me.

"Good thing we were both wrong," I said.

"Way wrong," she said back.

"For the first and only time in our lives."

"For real," she said.

I realized then that Cat counted on me just as much as I counted on her.

If not more.

Scene 54

Just when things felt better, like everything was finally okay, like it was a satisfying conclusion, Cat threw a question at me.

"What about Will?"

Will.

"He's a lost cause, let's face it," I said.

"Remember the tarot reading?" said Cat, like she was having one of those so-called lightbulb moments.

"How could I forget, even when I try?"

"Cassandra, she was right," Cat said.

"You mean about Will, Will and the death card?"

That's about all that stuck in my black-tar mind from that unpleasant memory.

"No, you took off, remember? She told me the death card wasn't about Will. It was about you."

"Me? So I'm the one who's going to croak? That could be the best news I've heard all millennium."

"No, listen to me. She said the death card isn't about dying in the physical sense. It's how something bad leads to something new and better. She said you'd have an emotional death."

"I feel the stake in my heart as we speak."

"But then she said everything would change, you'd have a rebirth."

I thought back on my own birth, the one where Will almost didn't let me out, where I almost never got to take my first breath. All on account of him getting in my way.

In the bottle-cap frame mirror over Cat's dresser I saw myself, a big fat mess. All scattered around every which way, nothing seeming to fit.

"What's that supposed to mean?"

"Listen, Sky, you have a second chance. You can relocate, find a new beginning. It's your choice, that's what she said."

"My choice?"

"You can start over. With yourself, with Will."

It made sense. Things couldn't go back. They could only move somewhere else. Somewhere safer, somewhere hopefully better.

It was up to me now.

Cat knew it, too.

"Go forth, do good work, Grasshopper," she said.

I gave her a gentle hug, careful not to break any more of her. Then I set out to figure out what would come next.

Scene 55

What better place to chart out my new life than the bomb shelter?

Quiet.

Serene.

Solitary.

The place to plan my renaissance, my rise from the ashes.

The holy temple of life underground.

Yes, underground.

Hey, lots of life starts underground.

Think about it.

Flowers.

Trees.

Grass.

Weeds.

Worms and parasites.

Ugh.

I lifted the door.

Sniff.

Shiver.

I smelled it. As in, nothing but trouble.

With a capital *W.*

Will. And his pot-smoking ways.

"Will?" I called.

No answer.

I pushed myself, moved halfway down the stairs.

The room was dark, damp, musty even.

Note to self: plug in dehumidifier. Clear the air. Do whatever it takes. Pronto.

Will was asleep on the futon (which luckily I had cleaned and sanitized to the best of my abilities), his arm covering his face.

So much for my solo retreat into the innermost sanctums of my soul-searching psyche.

At least until I give Will the boot.

I crossed to the futon, then kneeled down next to my brother, separating Will from the ashtray that held the evidence, the goods that belonged in a plastic Ziploc bag.

Tagged. Numbered. Labeled.

Your Honor, Exhibit One.

I found myself looking at him, an artifact, a specimen, an alien being.

I found myself questioning everything, interrogating it all.

I found myself being pulled back in time.

Will, you used to be fun.

You used to make me laugh. And vice versa, too.

You used to be there for me. I was there for you, too.

When did things turn so dark?

Who turned out the lights?

Then I saw Dad's face superimposed on Will's. Like one of those handheld holograms.

Will/Dad.

Dad/Will.

What's the difference?

I thought of what could have been. Of what would never be.

Listen up: your father left. He's never coming back.

Listen up: your brother is here. He still stands a chance.

I can help him.

Here I go.

"Will?"

No response.

"Will," louder.

Still nothing.

I shook his shoulder. His arm dropped from his face, limp, without life, a cadaver.

I rubbed the back of my hand against his cheek.

Cold. A piece of fake waxy fruit. A corpse in a casket.

"Will!" I cried.

I put my head to his chest.

Listen.

A faint heartbeat.

Barely breathing.

My own breathing pumped up the volume, stepped on the gas, my heartbeat, too.

"Sit up, Will, you gotta sit up, open your eyes, Will!" I cried. "Will, come back!"

I pushed him around. A sack of sand. Dead weight.

He was incoherent. Out of it. Too far gone.

ME: Too little. Too late.

Then it caught the corner of my eye. Silver.

Opened packets. Remnants of white dust. Count them. One, two, three.

Three blind mice.

Three blind mice.

See how they run.

On the floor, near the wall, a flicker of glass, an empty bottle, whiskey, keeled over on its side.

RIP.

Will.

Surrounded by lethal weapons.

Annihilated by weapons of mass destruction.

I tore up the stairs.

Into the house.

Dial.

9-1-1.

This is an emergency.

Yes.

Yes.

Yes, sir, it is.

Life.

Or death.

VIDEO DIARY,  ENTRY TEN

VIDEO: *MEDIUM SHOT of SELF who sits HALFWAY UP BOMB SHEL-
TER STEPS. SELF doesn't know if she should go up or down, back
or forth, in or out. SELF is dressed all in BLACK. SELF looks like she
is attending her own funeral.*

AUDIO: You might think I saved my brother tonight, but please
don't flatter me. I know the truth. The truth I don't want to face.
You've already had the history lesson. Simple. The more I got involved, the worse things got. Review the timeline. I failed him at
every twisty turn. And that's being kind. To myself. Let's be honest. Maybe I set him up for all of this. Maybe part of me wanted to
see him go down, so I could look better than him. So I could be
the good twin sister, the better half.

Just like he said.

Just like he said.

SELF breaks down, reaches out to camera, **SHUTS OFF***.*

SCREEN GOES BLACK.

Scene 56

Fast forward.

Three weeks later.

I would've come earlier.

Scout's Honor. Pinkie swear.

But.

No visitors allowed for the first two weeks. Intensive therapy. Focus. No distractions.

It's all about Will.

All about Will.

I sat in the Jeep idling curbside.

Check watch, digital: 9:50.

Tick-tock.

Tick-tock.

Check signage, yellowing paper behind glass:

> GREENWILLOW REHABILITATION CENTER
> VISITING HOURS 10 TO 2
> ONE VISITOR PER CLIENT
> NO CONTRABAND ALLOWED

I kept the Jeep running.

Fully prepared for a fast getaway.

Read my mind.

I was terrified of going inside, of being in a locked place.

Breathe.

I looked at the building. Sized it up.

Two-story. Brick. Hurricane-resistant.

Come in. We'll protect you. It's not so bad.

The perfect asylum in the event of an emergency.

Duck and cover.

We'll show you how. It's easy. Just like this.

Crouch down. Tuck in your chin. Cover your head with your arms.

You can do it.

Back to reality. The here, the now.

Repeat after me: Rehab. Rehab. Rehab.

Three times real fast.

rehabrehabrehab.

Louder.

REHABREHABREHAB.

Zoom in for extreme close-up.

Try to focus inside.

Figures, ghosts, shadows, floating past windows.

Plants desperate for air, pushing against smudged glass, saying, "Let us out. We hate it here. We need fresh air."

Why won't you help us?

Somewhere inside, Will.

I rolled down the window, stretched back, sucked back a slow swallow of molasses air.

Gag.

The red engine light flashed. I turned off the car.

9:59.

10,...

9,...

8,...

7,...

6,...

5,...

4,...

3,...

2,...

1,...

Blast off!

No turning back.

Time to go inside.

Scene 57

Hard cut to processing area. Start here, then proceed with escort to Visitors' Room.

Do Not Pass Go. Do Not Collect $200.

I showed my ID, signed the ledger. Name. Address. Relationship to patient.

Relationship to patient?

Twin sister? Twin sister who is also a friend? Twin sister who is also a friend who's a failure?

The space wasn't big enough. No room for telling all.

A brush-cut man wearing all white smiled, then said: "Here's your tag, miss."

I clipped the orange laminated badge marked "Visitor" to my jean jacket. *Phew.* Good thing. Now they can't mix me up with the patients. No mistaken identity. I get to go home when visiting hours are over.

Brush-cut man said: "Have a seat in the room next door, miss. We'll call you when someone's here to take you down."

I comply.

Dissolve to establishing shot from above.

A loony-bird's point of view.

Small room: white

Linoleum floor: white and black.

Cordless venetian blind: white.

At center: me, sitting alone. Old issues of *Outdoor Living* strewn around the table.

Zoom to close-up of my hands folded in praying position.

In the name of the Father,...

The Son,...

The Holy Ghost...

Me: wound up. Excitable. Antsy.

Grow up. Calm down.

Take a deep breath. Distract yourself.

Poster. Reproduction of "Vincent's Room, Arles."

Van Gogh, 1888.

Ms. Assenza taught us that one. She told us about the sliced-off ear. The mental torture. The living hell. The internal nightmare. The bullet to the chest that ended it all.

The inspiration every artist hopes for.

Welcome. Pleased to have you join us in this sterile diseased world of rehab.

Beautiful.

Claustrophobic.

Hopeful.

Terrifying.

"I can take you now, miss," said a lady with wire-rim glasses, stringy gray hair, a nice smile that you want so much to believe is real.

She was wearing an official name tag with a picture of her that looked like it was taken ten years ago.

Victoria. Victory. Victorious.

Okay, I like to pretend me and Victoria are on a first-name basis. It could make me feel more welcome, even a little at home. After all, why shouldn't I? My own brother is living here. At least for the time being.

I smiled back and got up, followed Victoria out of the room.

I listened to the jangling of Victoria's keys as I marched behind, each one of my footsteps like trudging through thick snow.

Scene 58

Victoria used her biggest key to open the heavy steel door to the Visitors' Room.

I stepped inside. Everything was battleship gray.

Even Victoria's eyes.

"Sit wherever you'd like," Victoria said. "He'll be right down."

Then Victoria sat behind a clunky teacher's desk, opened up a newspaper, took a sip of her coffee.

I liked how Victoria was doing her own thing, How Victoria wasn't paying attention to me. I finally started to relax.

I checked out my surroundings.

Above: recessed lighting. Too bright. Hurts to see.

Below: table bolted to floor.

Patient chair bolted to floor.

Visitor chair bolted to floor.

You're going nowhere.

Stay in place.

No false moves allowed.

The Dr Pepper I bought from the vending machine sizzled and overflowed when I unscrewed the plastic cap.

Did I do the right thing, having the authorities bring Will here? Could he have brought himself around with the aid of our friendly, neighborhood family practitioner? Could he have recovered at home? Could I have helped him do it?

A little TLC can go a long way.

I pressed the cold bottle against my hot cheek.

Relief.

I looked around.

On the far side of the room, a young couple was hunched together, holding hands, whispering.

Which one was the patient?

At the one nearest the door, an elderly couple (parents?) sat with a middle-aged son, playing cards.

Go Fish.

Don't stare. Never make eye contact. These are strictly private matters. Look down.

My right foot: *tap, tap, tap.*

Look up again. Everything is a little too nice. A little too perfect. A little too neutral, too antiseptic. Too sterile.

Get clean, get clean, get clean. That's what this place seemed to say. Loud and clear.

A wooden sign, hand-painted with old English lettering, was mounted above the big clock: "Greenwillow. A Safe Haven for All."

It made me think of the bomb shelter, how Mom used almost the exact same sales pitch when she first wanted us to get behind her crazy idea of digging it. The bomb shelter. It was supposed to protect us, keep us together, make everything safe and secure.

And look at us now.

Look at us now.

Scene 59

At the back of the room, a security door with a tiny letter-box window. Chicken wire sandwiched inside shatterproof glass. Just big enough for a set of spooky staring eyes.

Knock, knock.

Who's there?

Peek-a-boo.

I sit up straight, stiff, when I hear keys unlocking the big metal door. A man with laminated badges on a string necklace comes through.

The official escort. The usher. The maître d'.

Call him what you wish.

He opens the door, holds it open for Will.

I jump up, a jack-in-the-box.

I see the resemblance, he says.

My smile, jittery.

My heart, dry ice.

Will?

Will.

Scene 60

The grand entrance.

For once, his hair looked tame.

Or I should say, for twice.

Flashback to elementary school. Class photo day. First grade. I'm in line behind Will. Volunteer class mother combs Will's hair.

"Now, that's better," she sparkled, patting it even flatter with her hand while Will tried to spin around on the portrait stool. I bet she would've even spit on it if nobody was looking.

All for a picture that would look nothing like the real Will, a picture that would steal away the heart of who he really was. A picture he would never like, could never get used to, and the same went for me, too.

Fast forward to rehab.

Will is smiling. Happy to see me. A familiar face. A blast from the past.

Kiss, hug, hug.

"Hey, bro," I said, standing up to hug him.

"Hey," he said. It felt like he had come down a notch or five, like he had lightened up on the accelerator.

Something pulled inside me. It was all so hard to follow. I wondered about Will, questioned who he really was.

Would the real Will Baxter please stand up?

Then he smiled. And I knew for sure. The real Will was somewhere inside, trying to find his way out again. And right then, somehow I knew he would.

Will opened the ginger ale I had pushed in front of him.

"Cheers," he said, holding up his can like a New Year's Eve toast.

May auld acquaintance be forgot.

And never brought to mind.

"Yeah, cheers," I said. Then I smiled, too. And I toasted him right back.

His face had filled out. He was growing his first beard. Dark brown. Not red, like his hair.

Unexpected.

Defiant.

Out of control.

Just like Will.

Scene 61

He's wearing a gray sweatshirt, no hood, sweatpants, too baggy. Sneakers without laces.

No strings allowed.

Choking hazard.

No self-inflicted harm shall come to the inhabitants of this place.

Freeze frame.

Flashback with voice-over. The day the ambulance crew came.

E.R.

Third Watch.

Cops.

The day the two men in dark blue jumpsuits like astronauts picked up Will, strapped him on a stretcher, gave him oxygen, hooked him up to monitors, to an IV. Shoved charcoal down into his stomach.

Bloated him up like a water balloon.

Pop!

Mark your calendar.

The day they took my brother away. The day they locked Will inside, brought him to this secure place.

Thank you.

For helping.

Thank you?

For helping?

They seemed friendly enough. All business. You might say professional.

I noticed patches on their uniforms. Colorful. Authoritative. I thought about Boy Scouts and forest rangers and the reliable team at Valvoline Instant Oil Change.

Immediate trust.

"Where are your parents?" they demanded.

Is that a trick question? I felt like saying.

Mom is who knows where.

Someplace she won't have to deal with this.

Good timing, Mom.

Dad is who knows where.

Someplace with a new, improved family, for all I know.

Nice work, Dad.

"It's me. Just me," I say to the guy with dazzling white teeth.

"Can you fill this out?" he says back, handing me a form in trip-licate. "We'll reach your parents from the facility."

"The facility"? Why not "Retreat"? Or "Refuge"? Or "Friendly Neighborhood Sanctuary"?

Focus on paperwork.

Name.

Address.

Phone.

Social Security number.

It's all up to me, I told myself. I can do it.

In loco parentis, they told me.

It made me feel pumped up, important.

They handed me a felt-tipped pen. Black. Almost dried out.

I licked the tip, squeezed out the last of the ink.

I was going to make this happen. No matter what.

What good sister wouldn't?

Yes, I said, not in so many words.

Yes, my brother is beyond my help. Maybe even certifiable.

Yes, I'll sign on a dotted line.

The astronaut guys reminded me: We need to lock Will in. We need to lock the world out.

Not in so many words.

He meets the admissions criteria, not always easy, not always a given.

A danger to himself.

Check.

A danger to others.

Double check.

Congratulations, Will Baxter, you qualify.

It's that simple.

Take a seat.

Sit back, relax.

Congratulations.

Welcome aboard.

VIDEO DIARY,  ENTRY ELEVEN

VIDEO:. *SELF is in OWN BEDROOM. SELF sits CROSS-LEGGED IN BEANBAG CHAIR NEXT TO BOOKSHELF displaying vintage MY LITTLE PONY collection.*

AUDIO: If someone ever told me that someday I'd be visiting my own twin brother in rehab, I would've asked who spiked your Gatorade? Since Will's been away, I've had some time to think about him and me and Mom and the Dad-That-Never-Really-Was. I admit it. I used to think I wanted one of those ideal suburban lives, where everything is picture perfect, all neat and clean, inside and out. Who wouldn't? It would've been great to grow up with a real-deal dad and a regular kind of cookie-baking, rule-enforcing PTA-loving mom. Even the white picket fence, the two-car garage with the Grand Caravan parked inside wouldn't have been too shabby. How can I lie? But you know what? Nice isn't everything. Maybe it's the sticking together part that is. Everything, I mean. For sure, life isn't always a piece of Neapolitan ice-cream cake, but that's what makes it interesting. Even though it's hard. I hate that Will had to go through what he's still going through, and I wish I could know that we'll all have a happy ending, kind of like the ones in Mom's romance novels. Well, scratch that last idea. But leave in this one. We're all on our own crazy caravan ride, destination unknown. Together. For once and for all. Together.

WINDOW SHADE FADE TO BLACK.

Scene 62

Insert title slide: Two Weeks Later. The Homecoming.

"Welcome home, honey," Mom said to Will, patting his kneecap as we drove up to our house. I could tell she was a little hopped up, like she just downed a few too many mugs of Morning Thunder tea.

She bolted out the driver's side and scooted over to open up Will's door, putting her arm around his shoulder as he worked his way out. "Your room's all ready for you. I straightened it up this morning, put everything in its place."

I felt a gentle pull in my heart. I could tell from her voice she was trying hard, doing everything she could to make Will feel welcome, hopeful. She wanted a fresh start as much as Will and I both did.

It was strange, Will coming home from rehab. What do you do

when someone's released from detox? How do you think about it? How do you commemorate the day? It wasn't like he just returned from a safari or a business trip or a semester abroad. Something where there'd be a slide show to see, some postcards and brochures and pictures to pass around.

What could he possibly bring us for souvenirs? Straitjackets? Plastic eating utensils? Maybe a sedative or two? His next relapse?

Even so, we tried to make it feel like he'd been someplace good, like there was something to celebrate.

Which there was.

We were together, us three, walking toward the house, Will in the middle, Mom and me on either side. I was feeling hopeful, relieved for the first time in I don't know how long.

Then I looked up. Glanced over my mother's shoulder.

Look who's here.

Exact-a-mundo. Ed Dickey.

Mom cut him loose after Will went in rehab. She finally figured out he was pretty much the lame-o we told her he was.

Insert sfx: Hallelujah chorus.

We watched him walk up the driveway, then he stood there, arms folded, like he was self-appointed sergeant-at-arms, those auto-darkening glasses blotting out his beady eyes.

"Ed, I asked you not to come. Will just got here, we need some time," my mother said, a prickly irritation obvious in her voice.

"I just thought you might need my help, that's all," he said, frustration congealed with hopefulness. Pineapple stuck inside lime Jell-O.

"We're doing fine, just fine," said Mom, accentuating each word. Then she turned toward the kitchen door, started walking with Will, with me.

Ed took a step toward us, desperation setting in.

"It might seem that way," he said. "But look at what happened before, remember how far these kids can push you. Don't forget the damage they can do." He couldn't care less that I could hear. In fact, he seemed to be shooting his words in my precise direction.

Mom turned toward Ed's voice, then aimed her laser-beam eyes right at him.

She'd beat out the Cyclops in a staring contest any day. Hands down.

"It's time for you to go," she said in no uncertain terms.

His expression went soft.

"You're making a big mistake, Barbie," he said, like a big know-it-all.

"I'm afraid you've got the verb tense all wrong," she said. "I 'made' a big mistake is more appropriate. But I'm correcting the phrasing now."

"What's that supposed to mean?"

"Simple. Good-bye."

Ed's mouth stretched and snapped like a heavy-duty rubber band.

"Fine with me, if that's how you feel," he said.

And of course he couldn't just leave. He couldn't keep his big fly-trap mouth shut: "Well then, Barbie, you've just proven that apples don't fall far from the tree."

"Ed, one more cliché and I'm calling the police."

If Ed Dickey had a tail, it would have curled between his bony legs as he wimpered down the driveway and disappeared from our sight forever.

Scene 63

Will's left arm was a wet noodle around Mom as we walked him inside the house.

Still a little shaky. It's bound to get better. An uphill climb, the discharge planner told us.

I stood behind Will, my hand on the small of his back. I counted the ten steps to myself as he took them one by one, not three at a time like he always did.

He stopped on the landing while Mom flitted ahead to prop open the door with the phone book.

"A little fresh air never hurt anyone," she warbled. She was trying to keep the mood chipper, upbeat, and somehow I was feeling grateful for that.

"Sky, don't look so worried. Things are different now. I'm making a change, it's already made," Will said just to me. "You believe me, don't you?"

It sounded like he didn't believe himself. I turned to face him. His eyes were dark, ringed, sad.

I turned into him, lay my head on his chest. Gave him a one-arm hug.

"Sure, I do, you know that," I said, trying to turn on the cheer, to turn off the doubt.

"About the pocket watch, I don't know what I was thinking, that was so totally wrong," Will said. "I'm really sorry, Sky. For everything."

"It's all good now, don't worry," I said back.

We stepped inside. Mom was straightening up the kitchen throw rugs (the ones shaped like giant mutant veggies on steroids, of course).

"I'm calling the nurse. I promised to let her know you made it home okay," she said, punching in the numbers on her pink princess phone.

Wow. Sometimes you're actually on top of things, Mom. It's times like this when you really have it together in a good way.

I walked to the living room archway with Will close behind me.

I looked over at the red crushed-velvet loveseat.

"Hey there," beamed Cat, her leg elevated on the faux Dalmatian-fur footrest.

I glanced over at Mom, a quiz-show look on my face.

Mom covered the phone with her hand. "What's a homecoming without Cat?"

"I bribed her to let me come over," said Cat. "Three Kit Kat bars and a Yoo-hoo."

"My weakness," Mom said.

I gave Mom a thank-you look, then she took her hand off the receiver and went back to her call.

Will went right over to hug Cat.

"You're back," she said, her chin resting on Will's shoulder.

"For good, I hope," said Will.

"For sure," she said back.

Then I went straight over to hug Cat myself.

"So great you're here," I whispered in her ear.

"You think I'd miss this most momentous occasion?" she said back.

When I let go of her, I stood back, took in a panoramic view of us all.

How would I think about this, how would I remember my six-teenth summer? How would I summarize the major thematic threads?

Pan room.

Cat with her broken bones.

Mom with her broken dreams.

Will with his broken mind.

Me with my broken spirit.

But here we were, all of us together, each of us damaged goods in our own way. Maybe the imperfections were the glue that held all of us together.

Mom came in and sat next to me on the couch.

"I've decided to pursue a best-picture theme," she announced.

"A best-picture theme?" said Will.

"To give us focus, to get us back on track again."

"Best picture, as in Hollywood?" I asked, trying to give her most recent wacky idea at least a Casper-the-Friendly-Ghost of a chance.

"As in Academy Awards?" piped in Will.

Will and I traded the raised-eyebrow stare.

"I knew you'd be all for it. I've done some research and compiled a list of dinner recipes for each winning film."

"A recipe for each film?" I asked.

"Yes, the recipes should take us through the fall. And after today's kickoff meal, we'll start tomorrow with 'Wings,' Best Picture in 1927."

"Let me guess. Chicken wings?" Will said.

"Exactly. Teriyaki," Mom said, pleased as spiked punch.

And we all busted out laughing.

I realized then that some things will never change. And for the first time, I didn't mind at all.

"I'd better go stir the Crock-Pot," Mom said.

"Crazy Eights, anyone?" called out Cat. She started doing her fancy Las Vegas card shuffle.

I took another look at them all, then leaned back and smiled.

Scene 64

The last day of summer vacation.

MOM: Kids, listen up. I have an announcement to make.

Insert sfx: gavel banging.

The Baxter family meeting will now come to order.

Yes, in the backyard.

Yes, in front of a big pile of dirt.

Yes, beside a backhoe with a guy eating a sandwich perched inside.

And, yes, of course, at night.

ME: What now, Mom? Can you clue us in?

MOM: I'm having it filled in.

WILL: What? You have a cavity?

Will flashed that bright smile of his again. Luckily he got that back after rehab, plus his wise guy sense of humor, too. I sometimes worry that maybe this is only temporary, that the spiraling down is possibly just a sinkhole away, but for now, it all feels good.

I smiled back at him.

MOM: Yes, it is in fact a cavity, so to speak. It's the fallout shelter, that's what we're filling in. We've had quite enough, I trust you two agree.

I'd boarded up the bomb shelter in my mind weeks ago. The last time I was down there was the day I found Will. I hadn't set foot in there since. But still, the thought of filling it in, of covering over my sixteenth summer, pulled at my heart.

Maybe I wasn't ready for this.

"Remember you said it's the everyday experiences, the ones we take for granted, that give us structure, that's what we need to protect?" I said. "That's why you built it in the first place, right?"

"And what about Emeril?" said Will. "The way his show is so predictable, the way it gives you stability. You said it yourself, how important that is."

Mom didn't miss a snare-drum beat. "Emeril went out of my life when we got rid of cable. I've discovered it's more important to focus on the 'here and now' instead of the 'maybe and someday.'"

For once my mother was making sense.

What's happening to me?

I thought about Ed Dickey, the last love of her life who she dumped for once and for all. I remembered how relieved I was that she finally ditched him, how amazed I was by her strength through it all.

Hello, I'd like to introduce to you my-crazy-but-smart-and-sometimes-gutsy-Barbie-Baxter-red-wig-wearing-Nikki-Boudreau-romance-writing-insect-cake-baking-mom.

" What about all the stuff down there?" said Will.

The disco ball. The lava lamp. The chili-pepper string lights. Canned goods from A to Z.

"Consider them artifacts, for our sacred burial ground." Mom had obviously given this a lot of thought.

"I wonder what story archaeologists will piece together some-day about the Baxter family bomb shelter," I said.

"Excellent thought, Sky. We can only hope they appreciate our complexities."

I wondered how others would see my sixteenth summer.

Cat would say, "Sky, you made it, and so did I." Cat healed up, the cast came off. She and I still hang out on a daily basis, and she just started seeing this cool guy named Andrew who she met at the Enchanted Spirit. But guess what? It all balances out somehow. Her dad finally got work, and they moved closer, into a cute house in town. And even Susan cheered up a little. She quit Dunkin' Donuts and teaches aerobics now at the YMCA. It looks like she had a makeover.

Miracles do happen.

And Kurt. How can he be left out of my sixteenth-summer memory book? He started hanging out with Will again, and we're friends. We really are. After all, he's my first. And let's hope and pray he's not my last. There's still a little spark, but who knows if it'll ever ignite. For now, friends is a nice way to be.

Life is funny sometimes, the way it works out.

Or doesn't.

Back to the family meeting.

Will pulled up the door. We positioned ourselves around the opening like mourners over a freshly dug grave.

Mom said, "We need a ritual. That's what gives us substance, a personal history, a memoir. It's all about crafting a life."

"Where'd you get that idea?" I asked.

"I suppose I should credit *National Geographic*," she answered.

Okay, here we go again. *"National Geographic?"*

"Yes, I subscribed through Publishers Clearing House. The world views it provides are priceless. Who cares that we didn't win the sweepstakes? Children, we've reclaimed our lives. And that's the grandest prize of all."

I looked at Will. He rolled his eyes and smiled.

Some things never change. And for once I didn't mind.

Mom grabbed a fistful of dirt, then Will and I did the same.

Why not?

"We officially close this chapter. On the count of three," Mom said.

Will started us off: "One ..., two,..."

Altogether now: "Three!"

Then we tossed the earth up in the air, watching it fall and scatter into the bomb shelter like New Year's confetti.

Meeting adjourned.

As we walked back together to the house, I heard the backhoe rev up, but I kept looking forward. I never looked back.

VIDEO DIARY, ⚛ ENTRY TWELVE
(AKA, THE FINAL CHAPTER)

VIDEO: *Fade up to EXTREME CLOSE-UP of SELF.*

AUDIO: So Ms. Assenza, I hope you've enjoyed my sixteenth-summer video. I don't know if I can say I enjoyed making it, but the whole project was kinda like getting all the benefits of seeing a shrink, or reading one of those self-help books, or watching Oprah or Montel on a daily basis. So I'd say that's a wrap. This is Skyler Baxter signing off.

I made it.

It's been real. For sure.

Peace out.

VIDEO: *Fade to black.*